A Discriminating Death:
A Jane Brooks Mystery

By Susan Dorsey

Rainstorm Press

Rainstorm Press
PO BOX 391038
Anza, Ca 92539
www.RainstormPress.com

The characters depicted in this story are completely fictitious, and any similarities to actual events, locations or people, living or dead, are entirely coincidental.

No part of this publication may be reproduced, in whole or in part, without written permission from the publisher, except for brief quotations in reviews. For information regarding permissions please contact the publisher Contact@RainstormPress.com

ISBN 10 – 1-937758-16-8
ISBN 13 – 978-1-937758-16-5

Library of Congress Control Number: 2012937221

A Discriminating Death
Publisher: Rainstorm Press
Copyright © 2012 by Rainstorm Press
Text Copyright © 2012 Susan J. Dorsey
All rights reserved.

Interior book design by –
The Mad Formatter
www.TheMadFormatter.com

Design by: Eloise J. Knapp

This book is dedicated to
Emma & Miles

Acknowledgements

I am so thankful for all of the encouragement from my family and friends during the creation of this novel. My husband Michael, my in-laws George and Julie, my mother Vennah, and my sisters Rachel, Ellen, and Heidi were enthusiastic every step of the way. My aunt Janice graciously donated her time to edit and clean the final draft. I could not have finished this book without such overwhelming support from everyone!

I would like to thank the wonderful staff of Rainstorm Press, especially Lyle Perez-Tinics and my editor, Charlotte Emma Gledson. What an honor to work with such talented people!

Finally, I would like to thank my great aunt Bonnie Sage Ball. She wrote a book titled *The Melungeons (their origin and kin)* in 1969. She was at the forefront of Melungeon research in a time when racial views were beginning to change.

"Be good or the Melungeons will get you."
-Edward T. Price [i]

Chapter One

"Legends of the Melungeons I first heard at my Father's knee as a child in the mountains of Eastern Tennessee, and the name had such ponderous and inhuman sound as to associate them in my mind with the giants and ogres of the wonder tales I had listened to in the winter evenings before the crackling logs in the wide mount fireplace."[ii]

Jane brushed her sweaty bangs from her forehead as she pushed open the door to Bloom's Floral Shop. The air conditioning hit her like a wall of ice, and she breathed a sigh of relief. August in East Tennessee was almost as bad as deep winter. Either way, it was just misery to be outside.

She didn't see Annie behind the front desk, but she did hear a murmur of voices coming from the backroom that she and Rodney had converted to a temporary salon.

Jane was lucky and fortunate enough to know it. Not everyone had a chance to work with their best friends every day. Not only did she get to share a room with Rodney while their new salon was being built, but Annie had convinced them to set up their stations in the floral shop. Who would have guessed that Rodney's inability to go for more than three consecutive months without irritating salon owners to the point of being fired could be a good thing? And yet, she thought, as she walked down the short hallway, she was getting ready to start another day of work and there was no place that she would rather be.

She stepped into the salon room and heard Rodney gasp. "I cannot believe that woman had the gall to say that to your face. Kimberly, you simply cannot put up with that kind of attitude." Rodney gestured with a curling iron in his hand.

Jane saw Kimberly duck down in the chair as she answered. "I know! I told her that Mr. Wiggles deserved much better and that we would be finding a new groomer immediately."

Jane smiled to herself as she put her purse under her hair station. The room they were using was so tiny that she and Rodney had been able to listen to each other's clients' woes for a couple of months now. Jane was willing to bet that the Mr. Wiggles complaint was not going to be the most interesting of the day.

"Hey, Jane!" Rodney smiled at her. "How is the remodeling of the soon-to-be best salon in Knoxville coming along?"

Jane sat in her stylist chair and spun around to face him as he worked. Her first client of the day was scheduled well after Rodney's so she had decided to drive to the site and check out the progress before coming in. "So far, so good. I think they'll be ready to lay tile sometime next week which means we have to finally decide on a wall color."

"I can't believe how hard it is to pick a neutral," Rodney groaned. "I'm still leaning toward the Martha Stewart Homespun."

"That's too green. All of our clients would look sickly," Jane said. "I think the Desert Taupe is the way to go."

"That one isn't so bad. We need to check it with the tile though; it may be a touch too gray." Rodney put down his curling iron and picked up his hairspray bottle. He looked at

A Discriminating Death

his client in the mirror. "I never dreamed starting a business would be so hard."

"We still have the hardest decision to make," Jane said. "We still don't know what we are calling ourselves."

"You don't even have a name yet?" Kimberly gasped. "Aren't you guys planning a grand opening this fall?"

"It's Jane's fault we don't have a name. She simply will not listen to reason. Can you believe she just refuses to let me call it Rodney's Hair Palace?" Rodney smiled and winked at Jane.

"Oh, I'll listen to reason when you have something reasonable to say," Jane laughed.

"You two sound just like an old married couple." Kimberly closed her eyes while Rodney enveloped her in a cloud of hairspray. "Are you still living together?"

"Jane is still bunking at my house," Rodney said. "John and I aren't quite ready to throw her out just yet."

"Good thing." Jane stood up. "You can't get rid of me until the salon is finished."

Jane had enjoyed staying with Rodney and John. She loved Rodney and was looking forward to opening a salon with him, but she surely did miss living in her own home. Her house caught fire last spring. It had been devastating but really was a blessing in disguise. Her home was on Kingston Pike in an area that was rapidly being commercialized. The insurance money from the fire would allow her to build a salon in her downstairs while keeping the upstairs as an apartment for herself. She would have the shortest commute of anyone she knew. She and Rodney would never have to salon hop again. Things were finally going to be perfect. Well, things would be perfect once they decided on a paint color and named the salon.

Jane looked in her station mirror and saw her other best friend, and owner of Bloom's Floral Shop, enter the tiny room.

"You will never guess who just called and is coming in today for a consult!" Annie clapped her hands together and grinned.

Rodney did not even glance up as he unsnapped the cutting cape from Kimberly's neck. "Phillip and Cindy Restin are going to come for a funeral consult for their father's service." Annie's mouth dropped open. Jane wasn't surprised that Rodney knew what was going on; he had an uncanny way of knowing everything that was happening. She was surprised that the Restin Family was going to use Annie's small floral shop for what was going to be the funeral of the season. The Restins were as close to royalty as you could get in Knoxville. Annie was great at what she did, maybe the best in the area, but she was a one-man show, well, one-woman and her assistant.

"How on earth did you know that?" Annie demanded.

Rodney's client turned and looked up at him with her eyebrows raised. He held up his hands and backed away a few feet. "I promise I don't use a crystal ball, so don't even think about burning me at the stake. The explanation is simple. Bethany, Phillip's secretary, is a friend of mine. She called to invite me to a genealogy talk she's giving on Saturday night and she just happened to mention that Phillip and Cindy were going to call you to see if you could handle the flowers for the funeral on Friday."

"Of course I can handle the flowers." Annie frowned. "I've been doing the entrance displays for all eight of their restaurants for the past three months and I've never been late once. If they thought I couldn't handle large orders, they should never have approached me with the contract."

"That was Bethany too." Rodney helped Kimberly up from the stylist chair. "The Restins like to use small local companies and the florist they'd been using sold out to a large chain. You remember Griffin's Floral?" Rodney didn't wait for a response. "So, Bethany was here to get her hair done, liked your work and recommended you." He snapped the cape to remove the last strands of cut hair and pretended to bow toward An-

A Discriminating Death

nie. "You are very welcome."

"I didn't know that lead came from you," Annie said. "Thanks."

"I heard on the radio that James Restin finally died," Kimberly said. "It sure took him long enough, poor man. Imagine having a stroke and then just lingering all this time. I'd rather just flat out die on the spot." She picked up her purse and turned to Rodney. "My hair looks fabulous as usual. Don't forget to put me down for exactly six weeks from now."

"I will," Rodney promised as he walked her to the door. "And tell me who you find to groom Mr. Wiggles."

Jane thought back to what she knew about the Restin Family. It really was a big deal that Annie was going to do the funeral. The Restins had been in the area for hundreds of years; they were probably one of the first settled families way back in the days before Tennessee was even a state. Their real claim to fame though, was that they were absolutely, terribly, filthy rich.

The family had been big farmers and then one son decided to try his hand at selling farm equipment. He traveled all over the state before he got married and returned to Knoxville. Instead of going back to farm life, he opened a small restaurant on Gay Street in the early nineteen hundreds. Soon, business was booming. Jane knew all of this back history because every Restin Family Barbeque restaurant had the story printed in large letters on a side wall beside a huge picture of the founder. Jane thought it was questionable advertising as the photo did not really encourage you to make yourself comfortable and eat up, but it sure was memorable. The larger-than-life sepia image showed a stern-faced man with a long mustache, holding an octagonal pocket watch. His gaze seemed to follow you. Jane always felt as if he were staring at her while she was ordering. The watch made it seem as if he were telling her to hurry it up, people were waiting. Still, the marketing idea must have worked on some level because Jane had sure been in a lot of Restin Family Barbeque restaurants over the years. Their pork sandwiches and sweet potato fries were fabulous.

"I think it's great you're going to do the funeral," Jane told Annie. "Sit and let me fluff you up a bit before they get here."

Annie sat in the stylist chair while Jane plugged in her curling brush and went to work. Annie had been her client and friend for years now, and Jane knew every hair on her head.

Annie frowned in the mirror as Jane gently brushed her short dark hair. "I have some bad news for you."

Jane paused, her brush held in the air. "Spit it out. You need to tell me quickly before Rodney comes back in and tells me himself."

"I bet he doesn't know this little tidbit yet. The Restin funeral is going to be this Friday night at Sheldon Brothers."

Jane groaned. She had a date with Brian Sheldon this Friday night. There was no way he would be able to skip out on such an important service, not even if his brother agreed to work it. She had been seeing, or rather trying to see, Brian for a few months now. Apparently, the work schedules of a funeral director and a hairdresser did not often match up. It was easier to get together for quick lunches during the weekdays, but it was hard to set a romantic mood at noon in Panera Bread. Brian had finally kissed her on their last date almost a week ago and Jane had been dreaming of this weekend ever since.

"I know you're disappointed." Annie frowned again.

"Disappointed about what?" Rodney asked as he came back into the room. "What did I miss?"

"The Sheldon Brothers are doing the Restin Funeral on Friday night so Jane's big date is off," Annie explained as Jane spritzed her with hairspray.

"Ah, that is disappointing. Now I will have to bear the brunt of Jane's boredom on Friday. That will never do. Also, I'm just dying to know if he is going to kiss her again."

A Discriminating Death

"Hush, Rodney!" Jane frowned into the mirror. She really liked Brian, more than anyone she had ever dated before. No one was as shocked as she was when she fell for a mortician, but she had fallen, and fallen hard. There was just something about him that made her knees go weak.

"I can redeem your weekend." Rodney nodded knowingly at Jane. "Come be my guest at the fifth annual Genealogical Convention downtown on Saturday. The more the merrier."

"I don't know," Jane said. She tried to remember if Brian had mentioned any previous plans for Saturday. Maybe they could just reschedule their date.

Rodney saw the doubtful look on Jane's face. "No, really, come on! Please?" He clasped his hands together and pleaded. "John's working yet again and I need a date to this thing. How would it look if I showed up all by myself? Besides, Bethany needs our support. She broke up with her boyfriend last month and I hate to think about her all alone on a Saturday night. We can go hear her speak and then we can take her out to dinner on Market Square. We could go to the Tomato Head. I know you love their pizzas. Come, on, I'll buy."

Jane thought the idea of doing something with Rodney was better than risking being stuck in the house alone. "All right, I'll go."

"You won't regret it, I promise!" Rodney turned to Annie. "What about you? Are you interested?"

"I could be," Annie mused. "It depends on how wiped out I am after this funeral. I'll have to let you know later."

The bells over the front door jingled and Annie jumped to her feet. "I bet that's them. Wish me luck!" She straightened her shoulders and hurried to the front room.

As soon as she was out of sight, Rodney tiptoed to the door and shut it quietly.

"What are you doing? I have an appointment coming in five minutes."

"I need to talk with you in private." Rodney's voice lost its sing-song lilt, and his smile faded. "I have a problem and I need your help."

It wasn't like Rodney to be so secretive and serious. "Of course, I'll help you in any way I can." Jane meant it. She would do anything for Rodney.

"I think John is cheating on me and I want proof."

"What?" Jane's voice was loud with surprise. Rodney frowned and held his finger to his lips.

Jane lowered her voice to a whisper. "You must be crazy. John loves you! There's no way he would ever even think of cheating on you."

"I wish I could believe it, Jane, but I just can't. There are too many strange things going on. He works odd hours and won't answer his cell phone when I call him at work. Then, when I call down to the station, they just tell me that he's out on assignment or away from his desk." Rodney ran his fingers through his short brown hair. "I think he may be avoiding me."

John was a detective with the Knoxville Police Department; and if Jane knew anything for certain, she knew that John was devoted to Rodney. John was small-framed and quiet, while Rodney was large and loud. John was content to let Rodney take the lead in social situations and more than once, Jane had seen John sitting back and eyeing Rodney with admiration and love while Rodney went on and on about some local gossip. There was no way that John would be cheating on him.

"I'm sorry, Rodney, I just don't buy it. Maybe John has just been busy at work. He just recently got released from desk duty and maybe he's working extra hard to prove himself or something." John had been shot while trying to buy a sweet tea at a gas station early last spring. Rodney had enjoyed John being on desk duty while he recovered. Jane thought most of Rodney's anxiety sprang from the fact that John was now able to resume his normal duties.

A Discriminating Death

"Explain to me then why he will not wear the new shirt I bought him." Rodney's eyes flared, and Jane saw that he was seriously angry. "Salmon is his color and yet, whenever he leaves for work lately, he is always wearing the most drab, boring clothes imaginable."

"Well, if he isn't dressing up, then maybe he isn't seeing anyone else," Jane insisted. "Did you ever think about that? I've always heard you should worry when your spouse starts sprucing up and buys new underwear, not when they start wearing boring clothing out in public."

Rodney pursed his lips. "Maybe you're right. I don't think so, but maybe you are. It still doesn't explain why he's acting so strange lately. He's keeping a secret and I intend to find out what it is. I need your help, and Annie's too if she's up to it."

"What can we possibly do to help you?" Jane was almost afraid to ask.

"We need to tail him one night and see exactly where he goes. He'll spot my car, but maybe if we all kind of trade off, like in the movies, we can follow him without being too obvious."

Jane took a deep breath. There was no way she was going to be able to tail a police detective without him seeing her in the first few minutes and becoming very, very angry about it.

"I don't think that's going to work," Jane said as Rodney rubbed his temples. "Now hold on, I'm not saying that I won't help you. I'm just saying that there is no way John won't notice us tailing him."

"Hello? Are you ready for me?" The door opened slowly and Jane saw her ten-thirty client arrive. She pasted a smile on her face and patted Rodney's hand. "I'm ready, come on in Eileen."

She turned to Rodney and whispered, "Let's talk later, honey. I promise to help you figure this out."

Rodney took a deep breath and smiled before he turned to the door. "Hey, Eileen, did you see Margie in the parking lot?

She's my ten-thirty and if she is late one more time, I am going to do something terrible to her."

"Hold your horses!" Margie peeked into the back room. "I'm here. I was just a little distracted when I walked in. I never dreamed that I would see Phillip and Cindy Restin sitting in the front room."

Eileen waved Margie in and then shut the door behind her. "Me neither! I couldn't believe it when I heard it on the news, James Restin finally dead. I must say, his kids have made out well already. Who knows how much they got from that deal on the land between Townsend and Gatlinburg? They must have been sitting on a fortune. And now that James has finally passed on, they're going to inherit all the rest. It sure must be nice to be a Restin."

"Come on over here and let me get you started." Rodney held out his hand for Margie's purse. "You know I was just joking about doing something terrible to you. Now tell me about your niece's wedding. Wasn't it last week?"

Jane looked at Rodney. He acted as if everything were okay. She knew him as well as anyone did; if not for their hushed conversation, even she couldn't have guessed that he was worried about John. Who knows, maybe John was just as good at hiding things as Rodney.

* * *

Jane finished Eileen's haircut just as Rodney was brushing red hair dye on Margie. The smell was pungent, wiping away the usual floral scent of roses and carnations that permeated the building. Jane inhaled deeply; she loved the smell of hair color.

"Thanks again, Jane." Eileen held up a mirror and twisted around so she could see the back of her head. "It's perfect, as usual." She laid the mirror on Jane's station and reached for her purse. Pulling out several bills, she pressed them into Jane's hand. "I'll have to call you to confirm our next appointment. I may have to go to this conference in Chicago. I'm trying to get out of it, but I think I'm stuck."

Rodney handed Margie a magazine. He twisted an egg-shaped kitchen timer and set it on his station. "Okay, you've got twenty minutes. Do you want a Diet Coke?"

Margie shook her head no and flipped open the magazine. It was one of those trashy gossip magazines that Rodney subscribed to, the type that few people would admit to purchasing but that everyone read when they were waiting at the salon.

Jane walked with Eileen down the hallway and held the front door open for her. She shut the door quickly to keep the cool air from escaping and glanced toward the consultation table. Phillip Restin leaned across the table to grasp Annie's hand. Jane was too far away to hear what he was saying, but she clearly saw Annie's face blush bright crimson. Bethany, Phillip's assistant, was also at the table. She saw Rodney enter and stood up. Rodney walked over to her and had to bend down to kiss her cheek. She was barely five feet tall, thin and bouncy like the cheerleader she used to be. Jane smiled as she remembered Bethany admitting to having a crush on Rodney while he was playing football at the University of Tennessee. She swore she was devastated when he told her he was gay. Although they never dated, they had remained friends even after Rodney dropped out of college and started cosmetology school.

"Are we finished?" Cindy Restin tilted her head and assumed a serious expression. Jane could not escape the feeling that Cindy would talk to a small dog in the same manner as she addressed Annie. Jane instantly did not like her. It didn't help that Cindy was impeccably dressed. She was wearing a short black dress, large pearls and the kind of high heels usually seen on twenty-year-olds at night clubs. Her hair was perfect and her skin was smooth as porcelain. Jane thought that Bethany wasn't too fond of Cindy either; she noticed Bethany hadn't once looked at Phillip's sister.

Phillip turned and gave his sister a weary smile. Jane had seen pictures of him in the paper and had seen him on the news several times, but the media had not done the man justice. Wearing a tailor-made suit, he looked as though he just stepped out of a menswear magazine. He shared the same blonde hair and green eyes as his sister, but he looked more like a real person and less like the Barbie doll that Cindy resembled.

Bethany gathered the papers from the table and slid them into her briefcase. "I think we're through here, unless you have any more questions?" She raised an eyebrow in Annie's direction.

Annie was still staring at Phillip and it took her a moment to understand that Bethany was addressing her. "No, no. I don't have any questions. Don't you worry about a thing; the arrangements will be perfect."

Phillip flashed her a bright smile. "I'm sure they will be, but if you do have any questions or if you need to speak with me, please call." He pulled a silver card case from his jacket pocket and handed her a card. "Here's my cell number if you need to reach me directly."

Jane stepped back as the small group headed for the door. Cindy brushed by her without speaking, while Phillip made eye contact and smiled. Bethany paused long enough to examine a framed wedding announcement hanging by the front door.

"This is beautiful! I love the pressed roses." She turned toward Annie. "How on earth did you get the color to stay so vibrant?"

"My assistant Grace does our flower pressing. She doesn't let me in on all her secrets, so I have no idea how she keeps the colors so fresh. Rodney does the calligraphy for her. This is their latest work."

Jane watched as Cindy started tapping her foot loudly against the wooden floors. Cindy's shoes probably cost more than Jane would make in a month.

"It is gorgeous." Bethany smiled at Annie. "Your whole shop is beautiful. It's going to be hard for Rodney and Jane to come up with a more inviting atmosphere for their salon."

"Oh, Annie is going to help us out with the decorating." Rodney nodded at Annie. "She has quite the eye for beauty."

Annie blushed again as Phillip clasped her hand. "Thank you for all of your help. We are so fortunate to have you with us during this trying time."

Cindy opened the door and strolled out, seemingly undisturbed by the shimmering heat. Bethany and Phillip nodded once more and then followed her to the car.

Annie closed the door behind them and then turned and pressed her hands against her chest. "Do you realize this may be the biggest service of my career? Oh, it is such an honor to be working with the Restins."

Jane grinned. "Phillip, in particular, hmmm? I saw him hold your hand a little too long there at the end."

Rodney snorted. "Please! That man looks like a Ken doll. I wouldn't trust that fake smile for a minute."

Jane turned in mock surprise. "Why Rodney, I do believe you are intimidated by Mr. Phillip Restin."

"Oh, and you are in no way feeling intimidated by Cindy?" Rodney's eyes narrowed.

"Okay, you're right. She was just a little too perfect for my tastes."

"I don't know what is wrong with you two," Annie scolded. "Phillip and Cindy are two perfectly nice people who have just lost their father."

"And who have just given you a big fat check for floral work too." Rodney winked at her. "No wonder you like them."

Jane interrupted Rodney with a glare. "What's wrong with us is that we do not have an ounce of self-confidence when met with well-dressed, powerful people."

"Well, you both are going to have to get over it. With any

luck, I will be seeing more and more of the Restins."

"Especially Phillip?" Jane laughed.

The ringing of the phone kept Annie from replying. She merely scowled at Jane as she answered. "Bloom's, how may I help you?" Annie paused and then held her hand up to her mouth. Rodney looked at Jane and they both stepped closer to the front desk so they could hear the conversation.

"Oh Grace, honey. Don't worry about one thing."

Jane frowned. Grace, Annie's assistant, was supposed to be out taking the morning deliveries.

"Now listen up. I insist you go and get checked out either at the hospital or by your own doctor. The company insurance will cover everything. You can't be too safe. Promise?"

Jane opened her mouth and Annie held up her hand, motioning for Jane to keep silent. "Okay, no problem. I can get two more out this morning. Don't even worry about the arrangements. No, don't worry about the van either. Rodney or Jane will take me to pick up a rental during lunchtime."

Rodney looked at Jane and shrugged his shoulders.

"Okay, okay. Call me after you get checked out, honey. I'm glad you are okay, that's all that matters." Annie hung up the phone, looked up at the ceiling and took a deep breath.

"What's going on?" Jane asked. "Is Grace okay?"

"Grace was in a car crash. She was stopped at a light and the car behind her just plowed into the delivery van."

"Oh, no!" Rodney said. "Poor Grace! She could have whiplash. I had a cousin who was hit from behind while he was waiting at a stop sign and he had to wear a neck brace for months. What is she going to do about her wedding? She can't wear a big old neck brace down the aisle."

"Her neck is okay." Annie winced. "She hit her nose on the airbag. I insisted that she go and see a doctor."

"Really?" Rodney groaned. "The wedding is in two months. Her nose has got to be back to normal by then."

"I'm sure the doctor will set it or do whatever needs to be

done," Jane said. There was nothing they could do about Grace's nose. "How is the delivery van?"

Annie laid her head down on the countertop. Her voice was muffled when she spoke. "The van's back wheels are completely screwed up. The police had to call a tow truck to take it to a local mechanic. I can either have them fix it or tow it somewhere else. Until then, I have got to get a rental van. Thankfully, there were only two more deliveries left." She raised her head up and looked at Jane and Rodney. "Oh, I am going to need so much help from you guys. Not just today, but all week if Grace doesn't come back in. How am I ever going to get the biggest funeral of my life done and deal with all of this?"

"Now calm down, Annie." Jane reached over the counter and patted her friend on the back. "Rodney and I will help you however we can."

Rodney started to smile. "And you can help me too. I can't believe how lucky this is!"

Annie turned to him and raised one eyebrow. "What in the world are you talking about?"

"We can use the new rental van to tail John tomorrow night and finally find out if he has been cheating on me. There's no way he would recognize us in a rental!" Rodney's eyes widened. "Oh, do you think we could get a black van with tinted windows? That would really do the trick."

"Yeah, if the trick is for John to think someone from a government agency is following him," Jane said.

Annie froze for one moment before she spoke slowly. "I have no idea what you two are talking about. I'm sure there's a great story behind all of this, but right now I just can't think about it."

"That's okay." Jane patted her again. "Let's just get a van ordered and those last two arrangements made up before lunch. Rodney has a free hour at one. He can fill you in on all of his crazy theories while he drives you to the rental office.

We'll just take this whole thing one step at a time."

* * *

Rodney and Annie had finally left the shop. Jane was alone for the time being but had a highlight coming in at one-thirty. She used the time to straighten up the salon room. She thought about trying to clean some of the disarray that was Annie's work area, but decided against it. Annie was meticulous with her front room displays. Beautiful arrangements were displayed in Annie's ever-growing antique vase collection. She had won awards for her fresh and silk flower arrangements, but her work area was a complete disaster. No surface was left uncovered. Cut stems littered the floor, and buckets of flowers created tripping hazards. Jane had no idea how Annie was able to create such beauty from such chaos, but it seemed to work for her and Jane would hate to do anything that would cause Annie to break her stride when she had so much work coming up this week.

Grace called at one-fifteen and told her that the doctor confirmed a broken nose but was also worried about a slight concussion. She had recommended that Grace take it easy for three or four days before returning to work. Jane understood but wasn't looking forward to passing the information on to Annie. She and Rodney were able to help out somewhat in the floral side of the business, but they did not have the flare that Grace and Annie had. It took them a lot longer to complete even the most basic of arrangements. They were going to have to step it up and work overtime to help Annie out of this mess.

Jane's cell phone rang almost immediately after she hung up with Grace. She glanced at the caller I.D. and her heart skipped a beat when she saw Brian's office number. She knew he must be calling to cancel their date, but her desire to hear his voice overcame her disappointment and she answered on

A Discriminating Death

the second ring.

"Brian?" She hated how eager she sounded. It was like she was in middle school again.

"Jane, I'm so sorry, but I'm afraid I have bad news." Brian really did sound sad.

"I know. Annie told me that you have the Restin Funeral on Friday night. It's a big honor for you and your brother."

"It is, but I do hate that we have to postpone our date. Could we maybe make it up on Saturday instead?"

Jane realized that she was twirling her hair with her fingers and forcibly put her hand down on her lap. There was no way that she could cancel on Rodney now that she knew how upset he was about John. She sighed. "Saturday would be great, but unfortunately I've already promised Rodney that I would go with him to this genealogy conference downtown. He's suddenly into tracing his roots for some unknown reason, and John is working that night."

Jane could hear Brian breathing quietly on the other end of the line. "Do you think he'd mind if I tagged along? I've been sort of researching my family tree too. I have a great aunt who has done a lot of research and she passed the torch to me since she's grown older. No one else in the family was interested enough to take her papers, but I thought that somebody should make a record of our past."

Jane smiled and resisted the urge to dance a little. "I think that would be wonderful. Rodney will be thrilled to have some more company. One of his clients is giving a talk that night and then we had planned to go to dinner somewhere on Market Square. How about we meet here at Bloom's? Does five o'clock sound okay to you?"

Jane could hear the smile in Brian's voice. "That sounds great. I really wanted to see you this weekend and I sure hate how plans change. I was looking forward to Friday night."

"I think I might be seeing you Friday night after all," Jane said. "Grace was in a car crash and she's okay, but I think she's going to be out of commission for a few days. Rodney and I are going to try to help Annie get everything together before the funeral."

"That's very nice of you two," Brian said. "This is a big deal, for Annie and for us. I think it's wonderful that the Restin family is so supportive of small local businesses, but I am a little worried that our facilities might not hold all of the mourners. It will be a funeral to remember, that's for sure."

The front door opened and a brunette walked in and waved to Jane.

"Oh, Brian, my next appointment just arrived. I'd better go. I'll see you this weekend."

Brian paused and Jane held the phone tighter. "I'll look forward to it."

"Bye." Jane hung up the phone. She was thankful that she was going to get to see Brian this weekend, but once again it was going to be difficult to have a romantic moment while Rodney was blabbering away during dinner. She was just going to have to take what she could get. Jane deliberately put the thought of the weekend out of her mind and walked toward her client.

"Come on back and we can get started."

Chapter Two

"The simplest and most logical explanation for the name "Melungeon" is that the word derived from the old English term "malengin," meaning "mischevious intent." It was a word used in the works of John Gower, Sir Thomas Malory, and Edmund Spenser, works almost as well known in colonial America as those of Shakespeare."[iii]

"Well, I think it's a good idea," Jane said as she carefully finished straightening her client's hair. The flatiron was so hot that the hair would actually burn her fingers if she touched it too soon.

"I think it's ridiculous!" Rodney snorted. "The Restin development is going to be an Appalachian arts and crafts resort? Really? I bet everything they sell in the gift shop is made in China." Rodney kept his gaze focused on his client while he spoke to Jane.

Jane put down the flatiron and reached for the silicon shine spray. "I read in the paper that they're leaving the original Restin family cabin in place. It's going to be used for historical tours, living history classes and things like that. I think it's a fabulous idea."

Rodney groaned and turned his client to face him. "Do you believe what she is saying?" He gestured to Jane's station. "She really thinks that the resort is going to be more than just about money. I do pity her naiveté. An historical arts and crafts class held right next to a water park? Now that's the true spirit of the Smokies."

Jane turned to face Rodney and his client. "Come on, Rodney! There's plenty to appreciate about Appalachian folk arts. Most visitors to the area never really get an idea of what we're like or what we have to offer. This could help."

"I think I have to agree with Rodney about this one." Rodney's client smiled apologetically. "I mean, the resort is in business to make money. What seems to sell in Gatlinburg are those hideous black bears cut out of tree stumps. I highly doubt our ancestors ever did that."

Jane's client laughed. "Don't forget about all those hillbilly and moonshine figurines. I bet every northerner who comes down for a weekend has a hillbilly salt-and- pepper shaker or doorstop in their house!"

"Not you too?" Jane frowned at her client. "I know it isn't always vogue, but I'm willing to admit that I happen to like Pigeon Forge and Gatlinburg. Not all of it's campy. Have you ever been to the Gatlinburg Artists' Loop? There are some really talented people making local crafts up there."

"That's just the problem, Jane," Rodney's client said. "Think about the tourists that are going to stay at a resort like the Restin place is going to become. They'll never know about, much less care about, the Gatlinburg Artists' Loop. They're just going to leave and go home and think we all make moonshine and smoke corncob pipes."

"Oh, I don't know," Jane said as she ran her fingers through her client's hair one last time. "Maybe the Restin resort will be different. I sure hope so. Phillip seems like a classy sort of guy. Maybe he'll make sure it isn't a complete tourist trap."

A Discriminating Death

"Hope all you want, I promise you that I'm going to buy you a hillbilly ashtray from the Restin gift shop for your birthday next year." Rodney's voice was sing-song, and it irritated Jane. "Just you wait!"

Jane chose to ignore him. "There, you're all set." She handed a small mirror to her client so she could inspect the back of her hair.

"Perfect, Jane! Just perfect!"

Jane grinned as she accepted the payment from her first customer of the day. She loved Rodney hearing clients praise her work.

"And now, darling, you too are done." Rodney leaned down and smiled into the mirror.

His client stood up and handed Rodney some folded bills. "Do you think you'll have time to work my sister in next Thursday? She's always been jealous of my hair. She's up visiting from Atlanta and I figured the least I could do was to try to get her an appointment with you."

Jane pursed her lips a little as her client walked out the door. Rodney was obviously going to claim bragging rights for this morning.

"Just let me check the books." Rodney led his client toward the counter in the front room. He almost walked straight into Annie who was talking on her cell phone and practically running for the walk-in coolers.

"You simply have got to send me ten dozen more yellow roses by tomorrow morning! What do you not understand about that?"

Jane said good bye to her client and walked into the main workroom. She watched as Annie paced the small clear area on the floor. Annie kept her eyes straight in front of her but still managed to step around the various buckets of cut flowers littering the workspace.

"Thank you, thank you." Annie sighed and flipped her cell phone closed.

"I have the next hour free, and I am all yours. Jane reporting for duty." Jane saluted her friend. "Just tell me what you need done."

Annie's shoulders sagged. "I can't even begin to tell you what needs to be done! We only have today and tomorrow morning to get this whole thing together. Oh, I miss Grace like you can't imagine. She's going to be out of work until at least Saturday, and I'm not sure that I can make it until then." Annie sounded close to tears.

"Calm down." Jane stepped closer to her friend. "Now, I know we can't replace Grace, but Rodney and I are here and willing to do your bidding. Come on, tell me something to do."

Annie took a deep breath and tried to gather herself together. "Okay, let's check the incoming orders. Not only do I have the funeral flowers for James Restin, but every politician, business owner, local celebrity and every single person that has eaten in a Restin Family Barbeque restaurant is sending an arrangement to the service." Annie took another deep breath. "Everyone wants to pay their respects, and they want to make sure the family knows it."

"I can knock some of those out for you. Just give me the orders," Jane insisted, trying to ignore the mental image of thousands of arrangements spilling out the front door of the shop. It was going to be a long couple of days.

Annie walked over to a laptop that was wedged between two towering columns of bright green floral oasis. "Alright, here's what we have so far. Nobody is willing to send a cheap arrangement to the funeral, but at least half of them decided to send live plants. All you have to do for those is make a bow and a card."

"I am your live plant person then." Jane nodded seriously. "Rodney will be much better at the actual flower arranging. He has a couple of hours free right after lunch."

Annie pressed the print button and pulled off a stack of ten orders for Jane to complete. "Let me know if you have any questions," she insisted, her face as solemn as Jane had ever seen it. "Please print the cards carefully. I can't afford one single mistake."

"I've got it," Jane said as she flipped through the sheets. She walked over to the wooden dowel holding the bow-making supplies. Annie had taught her to make floral bows several months ago when she and Rodney had first tried to make themselves helpful in the shop. Jane figured that with all of the practice she was getting making elegant bows, her Christmas presents would be a thing of envy.

"Are you serious about coming tonight?" Jane asked as she pulled a length of burgundy ribbon from the roll.

Annie sighed again. "I did tell Rodney that I would help him, but it better not take up too much time." She paused and looked around the workroom. "I'll probably need a break by then anyway."

"It's really nice of you to let us use the shop's rental van on a wild goose chase." Jane picked up the scissors that were tied to the ribbon dowel. Left untethered, the scissors would have disappeared into the pile of cut stems and discarded petals long ago. "There is just no way that we are going to catch John in an indelicate position tonight. I think Rodney is scared because John is finally back on active duty."

Annie took a box of red long-stemmed roses to the work sink. She unwrapped them and began to strip the thorns and small leaves off at a furious pace. "I think Rodney is wrong too, but there's no talking him out of it. He has to see for himself." She cut the stems at an angle and put the flowers into a fresh bucket, ready for arranging. She turned and grabbed a box of white roses. "He explained everything to me yesterday while we were picking up the van. I'm sure there is an innocent explanation for it. This is John we're talking about, after all."

"He will never forgive us if he finds out we were following

him." Jane concentrated on pulling the bow loops out into a round shape and did not hear Rodney enter the workroom.

"Oh, he'll never find out," Rodney said. "How could he suspect that we'll be tailing him in that rental van? You ladies worry too much." Rodney walked over and flipped through the stack of orders. "Annie, I've got fifteen minutes till my next one; can I get started on these?"

"Get started on anything you can." Annie sighed as she grabbed the last box of roses. "There's a bundle of fresh greenery in the first cooler. It's right beside the baby's breath."

Rodney studied the order and then grabbed a glass vase from beneath the counter.

Jane finished the first bow and card, carefully printing each letter of the sender's name. Her handwriting was messy at best and when she wrote cursive, she herself often could not read it. She attached the card to a floral stick and picked up another order slip. For this one, she chose a deep purple ribbon. "I'll be glad when you see for once and for all that John is not running around on you."

Rodney frowned as he set the vase on the counter. "We will just see what we shall see. At least by tonight, I'll know. One way or another, I'll know."

Jane glanced at Annie. Annie frowned and went back to work.

* * *

"I cannot believe that we are really doing this!" Annie peered over the steering wheel.

"I cannot believe that you are not letting me drive!" Rodney leaned forward for a better view of the intersection.

"Well, I can't believe that I agreed to come along and sit in the back seat!" Jane laughed, earning disapproving looks from Annie and Rodney. "I mean, I might as well not even be here."

A Discriminating Death

"Hush!" Rodney ducked down in the passenger seat. "I see his car." They were parked at a gas station across from the main entrance to Rodney and John's neighborhood. There was always the chance that John would sneak off on a back road, but they decided to try the direct approach and watch for him to turn left onto Kingston Pike and head toward downtown or turn right and head for the smaller community of Farragut.

"Okay, stay low and I'll follow." Annie put the van in gear and edged closer to the road. She spied an opening in traffic and jumped onto the eastbound lane toward downtown.

"This is the way to the police station." Jane pointed out from her position in the back seat.

"That doesn't mean that's where he is going," Rodney hissed as he slid up into a more comfortable position.

The summer sun was still shining down even though it was after seven at night. Jane looked out of the side window and knew that if they had not had a rental van there would be no chance of spying on John. He might still notice them tailing him, especially if there was a miniscule chance that he was indeed hiding something from Rodney. His guilt might make him more alert to his surroundings.

They followed, keeping a two-car distance behind John's red Honda CRV. Unfortunately, a two-car distance in Knoxville meant that at least three cars would try to get between you and your target.

"He's headed for the police department." Rodney sounded disappointed. "Just keep driving past. We can park at Ruby Tuesday and see where he goes next."

Annie dutifully turned into the restaurant's packed parking lot and tried to find an open spot on the side near the police station. She had to settle on circling the parking lot slowly instead of maintaining a constant surveillance. Each time she passed the left side of the building, Rodney and Jane pressed their faces against the windows. "What if he stays for his whole shift, Rodney? I can't keep just driving around."

"I see him!" Jane exclaimed. She was getting into this spying a little more than she thought she would. "He's getting into a brown car."

"I see him too. Come on Annie, he's getting ready to leave." Rodney's voice was low and firm.

Annie drove once more around the building and then waited in the turn lane until they spotted John driving an older brown four-door sedan towards downtown Knoxville.

"He's going to be harder to follow now that he's not in his red car," Annie said. She glanced at Jane in the rearview mirror. "I won't be able to stay so far behind without risking losing him."

Jane leaned forward and peered out of the windshield. She had no idea what John could be doing ditching his vehicle for that rattletrap. She was sure that it wasn't going to be good, whatever it was.

Rodney was stone-faced and silent. Jane winced when she saw that he gripped the armrests of the passenger seat with fingers that had turned white from lack of circulation.

Annie darted effortlessly through the line of cars. She was a pro at weaving in and out of traffic. Delivering flowers for most of her life had made her fearless when navigating the congested Knoxville streets. Jane found herself tightly gripping her arm rests too as Annie pulled up behind John's borrowed car.

They followed John all the way down Kingston Pike to the Strip, a part of Cumberland Avenue beside the University of Tennessee. Annie slowed and allowed another car to slip in front of her.

"Okay, he's turning onto Seventeenth." Annie bit her lip and glanced at Rodney. He hadn't said one word since leaving the Ruby Tuesday parking lot. She put on her turn signal and followed the brown car through the intersection.

"Now he's going right on Highland." Jane was nervous. John was slowing down; he must be close to his destination.

A Discriminating Death

She couldn't imagine who he would know in the Fort.

The Fort Sanders community was a mixture of modern condos and turn-of-the century homes that had been converted into apartments to house the multitude of college students all wanting to live within walking distance of campus. There were a few neighborhood businesses, mostly cheap diners and small restaurants specializing in ethnic foods.

They saw John pull into a parking spot on the opposite side of the road. Rodney and Jane both ducked down in their seats this time as they drove past him. Annie pulled into an apartment parking lot one building down from John, the front of the van angled away from John's line of sight.

Jane looked out the tinted back window and watched John dart across the busy street. He walked up the front steps of an older, rundown house. The paint had once been white but was now peeling from the wooden siding. The row of dinged mailboxes announced that somehow the owner had been able to convert the single family residence into five separate apartments.

Rodney and Annie turned in their seats to watch with Jane. John stood underneath a large unmoving ceiling fan on the front porch. He looked up and down the street before hammering a brisk knock onto a faded green door marked with a slanted number two. The door immediately opened and John walked into the darkness.

"That's it," Rodney whispered as he unbuckled his seat belt and opened the van door. "I'm going after him. He has some explaining to do."

Jane was scared by how flat Rodney's voice was. She quickly unbuckled her belt and jumped out of the van. She grabbed Rodney's arm and pulled him back behind the van, blocking him from sight of the rundown apartment building. "Wait just a minute! You want to know what's going on? Let's just watch and see."

"You two get back in here right now!" Annie's whisper

was urgent. "There are more people going in."

Rodney paused in confusion. Jane's heart hammered against her chest as she turned him around and physically pushed him back into the van. She climbed in after him, scraping her knee on the rough carpet covering the floor. She pulled the door shut and scooted to the back. Thankfully the last two rows of seats had been removed and they could easily kneel to look out the back window. Jane shifted her weight off her stinging knee as Annie crawled out from behind the steering wheel and joined them.

"There are two more." Jane spied two scruffy-looking men in their early twenties knocking on the door. It quickly opened and they too disappeared into the shadowy interior.

"What in the world is going on?" Rodney spoke slowly as though trying to process too much information.

"At least it's obviously not a romantic tryst." Jane saw a group of three women approach the door next. "I told you that you don't have anything to worry about."

Rodney's eyes narrowed as he turned to look at her. "He may not be having an affair, but he is keeping secrets and I intend to find out exactly what he is up to."

"Don't even think of going back out there," Annie hissed. "It was hard enough to tail him once. There's no chance we will ever be able to do it again. Now let's just be quiet and wait to see what happens."

* * *

After an hour and a half of waiting, Jane was ready to call it a night. She was miserable. Annie had refused to keep the van's motor running after it became obvious that John was going to be more than fifteen minutes inside. They rolled the windows down and were able to catch a small breeze, but the August heat still made the van feel like an oven. Jane's hair stuck to the back of her sweaty neck as the sunlight slowly faded. Her

A Discriminating Death

legs kept falling asleep from sitting in a cramped position against Rodney, who, by the way, didn't smell very fresh in the heat, and she was hungry too. No one had thought to bring snacks to the stake-out, and she knew she was going to have to find a bathroom sooner rather than later.

"It's getting almost too dark to see," Annie said. Jane jumped at the sound of her voice. She had assumed from the tilt of Annie's head and her relaxed breathing that she had fallen asleep at least thirty minutes ago.

Rodney didn't even flinch. He continued his glaring at the apartment door, reminding Jane of a cat crouched outside a mouse's hole. "There's plenty of light from the streetlights. I can see just fine."

"Be that as it may," Annie yawned. "We've been here long enough. We know where he went. That is what you wanted to find out, right?" She rubbed her eyes. "There's nothing else to learn here tonight and we have a big day tomorrow –"

"Wait! He's leaving!" Rodney interrupted Annie with an excited whisper. "Look, there he is!"

Jane and Annie peered out the back window again and saw John standing on the sagging front porch. He was waving to a couple of guys who were bounding down the steps laughing and smiling. A breeze carried the sound of their laughter into the van.

"It looks like he had a good time," Annie said softly.

A thin woman with green spiked hair came out of the apartment. She was wearing combat boots, cut-off jean shorts and a tank top. Even from a distance, Jane could see her arms and legs covered with dark tattoos. She waved to the two men on the sidewalk and then wrapped her arms around John and drew him into a long kiss.

Jane cringed as Rodney gasped beside her; he sounded as if he had been punched in the stomach. She reached out and grabbed his shaking arm. "Let's go. Let's go home. Do not go out there. Do not."

He turned to her, and she shrank back from the look of pain on his face.

"Oh Rodney, we don't know what it means, okay? Let's just go home and wait on him to explain things. There has to be an explanation. There just has to ..." Jane trailed off, wondering what explanation John could possibly give for such treachery.

Annie was already climbing into the driver's seat. "Come on and buckle up, we are out of here."

Rodney watched, frozen in place, as John kissed the woman one more time, this time a quick kiss on the lips. Annie pulled out of the parking lot and was headed for the interstate when he took a deep breath and settled himself silently into the front seat.

***

Jane could hear Rodney quietly crying after Annie turned off the engine in the parking lot of Bloom's. Annie sighed, unbuckled her seatbelt, and reached over to hug him. Jane slowly unbuckled her belt too. She looked at Annie patting Rodney's back and murmuring soft words to him and felt sick. She could never have imagined in her wildest dreams that she'd have to drive Rodney home to confront John tonight. It seemed simply impossible for John to be cheating on Rodney, and with a woman no less. If Jane had not watched it with her own eyes, she would never have believed it. Why, Jane couldn't have been more surprised if she had seen John sprout wings and fly. She could only imagine the shock that Rodney felt.

Rodney took a deep ragged breath and rubbed his eyes. Annie glanced questioningly at Jane in the backseat. Jane met her eyes and nodded once before she climbed out of the van and into the humid night air.

"Come on Rodney, let's get you home." Jane opened his door and placed her hand on his arm. "Come on."

A Discriminating Death

Rodney straightened up and cleared his throat loudly. "Okay, I'm ready." He looked at Annie and smiled sadly. "Thank you for driving us tonight. It's terrible, but I would rather know the truth than live with any more lies."

"Now, you still don't know the truth." Annie frowned. "You just know what we saw, and I for one can't believe that there isn't something else going on here."

Rodney got out of the van slowly. "Seeing is believing, Annie. Trust me, I've seen enough."

Jane unlocked her car and watched Rodney settle into the passenger seat; he was moving like a man twice his age. "We'll see you in the morning, Annie. We'll be here bright and early to help out with the rest of the arrangements."

Annie hugged Jane. "Take care of him and let me know what happens. I just still can't believe it."

"I don't believe it either," Jane admitted. "There has to be more to it, but I have no idea what John could say to make any of this better."

* * *

The motion-activated outdoor lighting flooded Rodney's yard and driveway with blinding light as Jane pulled in. Living with a detective meant some serious home security. Jane had to buy black-out curtains for the guest bedroom after she moved in because every stray raccoon or possum would trip the motion sensors and light up the sky, interrupting her sleep at least three times a night.

She parked at the end of the driveway and pressed the remote to open the garage. John's car was not parked in his usual space. Jane exhaled, relieved that the confrontation was put off for at least a little while longer. She and Rodney walked slowly up the stairs into the large modern kitchen.

Rodney went straight to a small wine rack over the microwave. "Let's see here. What goes well with a cheating spouse? How about a nice Pinot Noir?"

Jane reached for the wine glasses. "I think that sounds just right." She placed them on the counter as Rodney stared at the corkscrew in his hand. It had a silver tree on the handle. Jane knew John had given it to Rodney with a ridiculously expensive bottle of wine for their third anniversary. "Do you want me to stay here while you talk to John or do you want me to make myself scarce?"

"Oh, please stay. I don't think I can do this alone." Rodney's voice trembled as he opened the wine.

"Okay, whatever you want," Jane said. She saw Rodney's eyes widen with fear at the sound of the garage door opening. John was home.

Jane held her breath while Rodney poured two glasses of wine, his hands shaking so badly that the red wine spilled over the counter. Jane looked around the room as she heard John's footsteps on the stairs. She grabbed her wine and quickly sat down at the table, choosing a chair near the door in case she needed to leave in a hurry.

Rodney leaned up against the counter and drank half his glass in one swallow. John entered the kitchen and Jane could see his expression instantly change as he felt the tension in the room.

"What's going on?" John stepped forward and looked at Rodney with concern. "Have you been crying?" He spun around to face Jane. "What's wrong?"

Rodney surprised Jane by keeping his voice from quivering when he spoke. "What is wrong is that I know the truth. I know all about your late-night excursions and I sure know about that tramp you were kissing on the front porch of her skanky, run-down shack this evening." Rodney swirled the remainder of his wine in his glass and then took a long sip, keeping his eyes on John's face the whole time.

Jane shrank back in her chair. John froze for a moment and then his shoulders sagged. He pulled out a chair and sat down heavily beside Jane. "How do you know?"

Jane's mouth fell open. She was shocked he didn't at least try to deny the allegations. She had expected him to be outraged, not defeated.

Rodney blinked back tears and stared at the ceiling for a minute as he took several deep breaths. "I know because we followed you tonight. Annie and Jane and I saw everything. At first I couldn't believe my eyes, but now that I know you've been sneaking around on me, I'm amazed I didn't see the signs before."

"Sneaking around on you?" John sat up a little straighter. "I was not sneaking around on you. How could you ever think that? Especially with a woman?"

"Oh, let's see. Maybe, because you were kissing her?" Rodney slammed his wine glass down on the counter, snapping the stem in two.

John turned to Jane. "I expect wild accusations and crazy behavior from Rodney, but Jane? What were you thinking to let him talk you into following a detective on active duty?"

Jane longed to bolt from the room. The fact that John was no longer acting like a disgraced lover did not seem to help the situation at all.

"She was helping me out because she is my true friend. She is loyal. Oh, I forgot, you don't know the meaning of that word." Rodney started to walk toward John, stopped and placed his hand over his eyes. "Did you say you were an active police detective? Is that what you just said?"

John stood up, pushing the chair back under the table so hard that it fell over. "Yes, an active police detective. As in, I am back on active duty and you need to stay away from my job." John shook his head in amazement. "You could have blown everything for me back there. Months of work could have been lost because of your stupidity and jealousy. What were you thinking?"

Rodney's eyes flashed with anger. "I was thinking that you

were hiding something from me. I was thinking that you were keeping secrets, skulking around at odd hours, not answering your phone. And I was right, wasn't I? You may not be sleeping with that trash, but you sure did lie to me. I don't think I can forgive that."

Jane felt sick. Rodney had suffered from terrible nightmares after John was shot last spring. The frequency of the nightmares had dropped after John had been relegated to desk duty during his recovery. John had told them he had a couple of big projects to finish up before he would go back on the duty roster. Rodney was dreading that day, and Jane knew Rodney expected John to tell him when it actually happened. This was a real betrayal of Rodney's trust. It was going to take a miracle for him to forgive John. She didn't doubt that Rodney's nightmares would start up again tonight.

John looked at Rodney and lowered his head. "I know you're angry with me, but don't you understand? I couldn't tell you or anyone," he said, as he glanced at Jane. "I couldn't tell anyone what I was working on. I wasn't trying to lie to you."

"What are you doing?" Rodney whispered.

"I'm not back at my old position yet, but I am on active duty. I'm undercover. For the first time in my career I get to do an undercover assignment and my lover and his best friends spy on me. Fabulous."

"Undercover?" Rodney frowned. "That's riskier than being on the roster, isn't it? Don't I have the right to know if my partner is putting himself in danger? What's the assignment? You have to tell me everything."

John raised his hands in frustration. "Rodney, that is the whole point of being undercover. I can't tell you anything, much less everything. You, especially. I mean, it is supposed to be a secret assignment, not something to be gossiped about over haircuts."

Jane winced. John had a point there. Rodney could keep a

secret for about three minutes, maximum, and then it was over. You might as well put it on a billboard in downtown Knoxville; just as many people would know the news.

"I don't like this," Rodney growled. "I didn't like you being a detective, but I like this even less. I can't stand the thought of you out there somewhere doing God knows what while I wait at home in the dark." Rodney's eyes narrowed and he raised his finger to poke John in the chest. "I have a right to know if you have been kissing anyone else before you kiss me. When were you going to tell me that information, huh? Oh, no, no, no." Rodney held up his hands and stepped backwards. "This is not going to work. Now tell me exactly what you are doing with that skank."

John straightened up and glared at Rodney. Jane knew the effect was lost on him. John might be the police detective and carry a gun, but he stood a head shorter than his hairdresser partner.

"I am not going to stand for this!" John actually spat at Rodney a little bit as he leaned closer to him. "Now you listen, and you listen good. I know you are scared for me, and I appreciate that, but you will keep your nose out of my business. If I ever hear that you have tried to follow me again, or in any way interfere with my investigation, then I will have no choice but to arrest you on obstruction charges. Do I make myself perfectly clear?"

Rodney took a deep breath and Jane grabbed the sides of the kitchen chair, bracing herself for the worst. Instead of shouting back, Rodney pressed his lips tightly into a thin line, turned and walked quietly out of the kitchen. Jane looked wide-eyed at John as they heard the master bedroom door slam shut, rattling the house.

John turned to Jane as his shoulders sagged. "Do you understand, Jane? Please tell me you'll help with Rodney." John walked to the cupboard and pulled out another wine glass, carefully avoiding the broken glass on the counter. He took the bottle and the glass and sat down at the table.

"I just don't know, John. Rodney was really hurt tonight. Seeing you kiss that woman was just terrible."

John flashed her a quick smile as he refilled her glass. "Just imagine having to do it. Now, that was terrible." He filled his glass and took a sip. "I know I should've told Rodney that I was starting undercover work, but you know how he is. He would've worried and stressed and badgered me nonstop. I didn't want to put either of us through that."

Jane slowly twirled her wine glass in small circles. "I can understand that, but Rodney finding out like this? It's going to take a lot of work to repair his trust."

John's face hardened slightly. "He's going to have to trust me, and you do too, Jane. I am serious about this. This group I'm investigating is pretty hardcore. A lot of work has been done to get me in and there could be serious consequences if they find out I'm a cop. Promise me that you'll tell Annie to back off and that you two will help Rodney keep his nose down. I don't want any of us to get hurt."

Chapter Three

"The old grannies say that one time Old Horny got mad at his old shrew-wife and left Hell and wandered all over the earth till he reached Tennessee. He set on a high bald and looked around him. "I declare to Creation," he says. "This place is so much like home, I just believe I'll stay awhile." So Old Horny found him an Injun and started in housekeeping....

And they do say it was those off-spring of Old Horny that growed up and started the Melungeon kind."[iv]

    Jane sipped her second cup of coffee and flipped through the pile of orders again. She was exhausted. She had been way too hyped up to go to bed at a decent hour last night, and when she did finally fall asleep well after midnight, she was awakened by the sound of Rodney crying out in fright.

    Only once had he ever told her the details of his nightmares. He always dreamed that he was at a funeral and was trying desperately to push his way through a large crowd so that he could see the casket. Finally, he would open the lid and look down to see John's bloody and battered body. Jane knew the nightmare had returned. She got up to go to him, but by the time her hand was on the doorknob, he had quieted down.

Jane waited for another minute and then climbed back into bed. John was sleeping on the sofa, and she did not want to wake him if Rodney's cries had not.

John had been gone by the time Rodney and Jane were up. They had a quick bagel and drove to the floral shop two hours before their first appointments so they could help Annie.

Jane glanced at the clock. She now only had half an hour before her first client and there were still more orders to fill. Annie's hair was sticking up in all directions as she flew around the workroom. Earlier, she had called to check on Grace, who had begged to come in and help Annie get ready for the service. Annie had flatly refused; Grace was not to come near the shop until she was completely over her injuries. All three friends had offered to help Grace with anything she needed during her recuperation: meals, errands run, anything. Grace had graciously turned them down. Her fiancé was serving overseas and was not able to be by her side, but her soon-to-be mother-in-law had firmly taken her under her wing.

Rodney worked on a large mourning wreath and told Annie all about John's deception, his undercover work and his demand for secrecy. Annie swore she knew all along that there had to be an explanation. She encouraged Rodney to forgive John; the simple truth was that part of this job would have to be kept secret from Rodney and everyone else. Rodney had waved a lazy hand at Annie and said that he was not ready to forgive John yet.

The three of them had worked the rest of the time in silence, hurrying to complete orders as quickly as possible. Jane sized up the dwindling pile of order forms; they were making pretty good progress but there was still a lot of work to be done.

Annie sat down on a stool with a faded vinyl cover. She blew her bangs out of her eyes and looked at her friends. "Thank you both so much for all of your help this morning. I swear, I don't think I could get through this without you."

"We are happy to help," Rodney said. "It's nice to keep busy and take my mind off things, you know?"

"Are y'all still going to be able to help me deliver and set up at five tonight? I don't want to knock you out of any appointments."

"We're all set. I moved a couple of people yesterday and everybody was fine when they found out it was because we were helping you with the Restin funeral. It seems as if everyone in town liked that man."

"It also seems as if everyone in town ordered an arrangement." Annie reached for a bucket of yellow roses and started to peel the damaged outer petals off the blooms. "I'm going to have to take at least one load over about three and then head back here to get freshened up and take you guys to unload the big sprays. Can you man the phones while I'm gone?"

"Sure, no problem, Annie. We have it under control." Jane put another bow on a floral pick and stuck it into the moist soil of a potted lily.

"For heaven's sake, just don't take any more orders for the service," Annie laughed.

Jane heard the sound of the bells over the front door ringing and she wiped her hands on her green work apron. "I'll go see who it is."

She walked through to the reception area and waved at a silver-haired woman who was admiring a silk arrangement beside the cash register. "Good morning, Reba, I'll tell Rodney you're here."

Rodney leaned through the doorway and grinned at his client. "Why, Reba, are you sure your appointment is today? You look fabulous. You know I can't improve on perfection."

Reba blushed and laughed. Jane rolled her eyes.

* * *

Jane walked her last client to the door and saw Annie parking the rental van. She stepped outside to wait on Annie and was almost overcome by the smell of hot asphalt wafting in shimmering waves off of the parking lot. She could hardly wait till October; it felt like the cool autumn breezes would never arrive.

Jane held the door open as Annie trudged up the steps. "I sure hope you have time to fix me up a little bit. My make-up has melted off, and I know my hair is a mess."

"Sure thing, just let me grab a Diet Coke."

"Make it two." Annie sighed as she headed toward the salon room.

"Make it three," Rodney called out as he walked his client into the front room. "I need a little more caffeine to get me through the next few hours."

"Maybe I'll see you all tonight." Rodney's client patted him on the shoulder. "I'm going to the funeral too."

"I think there's going to be quite a crowd," Annie said.

Jane squeezed past Rodney and headed to the workroom to grab three cans from the shop's fridge. Annie was already seated in the stylist chair by the time Jane got back. She handed a can to Annie and set one on Rodney's station before she opened her own.

"Okay, work your magic," Annie said.

Rodney walked in, his shoulders visibly slouched now that his client had left. Jane could not imagine how he had been able to keep up his happy-go-lucky persona all day. Not one of his clients had guessed that something was terribly wrong. Jane thought it was ironic that as much as Rodney liked to gossip about other people, he sure kept his own business close to his chest.

He sat down heavily in his chair and spun in slow circles while Jane grabbed the curling iron and gently turned under the ends of Annie's hair. She had cut it in a short bob last week, and it framed Annie's face beautifully, her dark hair setting off her blue eyes.

A Discriminating Death

"Did you leave our change of clothes in the car?" Rodney asked.

"No, I put them in the hall closet." Jane sprayed Annie with a gentle-hold hair spray that smelled like coconuts.

"I'm going to go ahead and change, then." Rodney grabbed his drink and wandered out of the room.

Annie looked at Jane with concern. "Did he ever talk to John today?"

Jane shook her head and frowned. "No. He had his phone turned off, so who knows if John even tried to call?"

"I kind of expected John to come by the shop, you know? I thought maybe he would be ready to kiss and make up."

Jane's frown deepened. "No, John was pretty angry last night. He was adamant that Rodney take the undercover assignment seriously."

"They are going to have to work it out soon." Annie stood up. "I can't imagine them not being together."

"I agree. I always thought they would be together for the long haul." Jane ran her fingers through her hair and reached for the bottle of root booster to give her some more volume.

"I'm going to touch up my make-up and change clothes." Annie moved so Jane could see herself in the mirror. "I think we only have a spray and two wreaths to fit in the van this trip. Can you be ready to go in ten minutes?"

Rodney walked back in, now wearing a charcoal suit with a cream-colored shirt and deep purple tie. He picked up the broom and dustpan. "I'll clean up in here while you two change."

"Thanks, Rodney." Jane unplugged her curling iron.

"I'll do my make-up here and you can change in the bathroom first," Annie said.

"Give me five minutes." Jane finished her drink and went to change. With her auburn hair and pale coloring, she looked good in black. Her closet was full of clothing that she could wear to a funeral, not a bad thing now that she was dating a mortician.

She changed and then touched up her own makeup while Annie dressed in the bathroom. Jane was excited about getting to see Brian tonight, even if he was working. It was better than nothing, and when it came to Brian she had learned to take what she could get.

They loaded the arrangements with minimal trouble. Jane was stuck holding the folding frames for the wreaths across her lap in the back seat of the van, but everything else fit nicely.

Annie was able to get them to the funeral home by five thirty, despite the interstate's daily transformation into a parking lot as everyone in Knox County tried to leave work and head home.

They had a little over an hour to finish the set-up before the service started, but already the parking lot was starting to fill up. Annie pulled the van around to the back of the funeral home and parked near the office entrance.

They took the arrangements up in two trips and had just draped the casket spray over the bottom half of the open casket when Brian and Phillip walked into the room.

Jane was delighted to see Brian's eyes light up when he saw them. She tried to keep a smile off of her face as they walked closer. She sure didn't want Phillip thinking she was happy to be at his father's funeral.

"Jane, Annie, Rodney!" Brian reached Jane's side first and clasped her hand in his.

Jane saw Phillip stand beside Annie and place his hand on her back. He leaned in toward her. "The flowers are beautiful. You've done an amazing job. Dad would be so pleased." Annie blushed. "I had a lot of help from these two." She nodded toward Jane, who was still holding hands with Brian, and Rodney, who was looking at his feet. "I don't know what I would have done without them."

The door opened again. Bethany stood in the doorway and

motioned for an older man to enter. "He's over here."

Phillip kept his hand on Annie's back as the stranger approached.

"Henry Atkins." Phillip nodded toward the older man. "Please meet my friends Annie, Rodney and Jane. You've met Brian Sheldon already, haven't you?" Phillip looked at Annie. "Henry is our family attorney. He helped Dad determine his funeral plans several years ago and has handled everything so smoothly since Dad passed."

Henry's voice was gruff and Jane could imagine him sitting in a leather chair somewhere smoking a pipe. "I think everything has gone as James would have liked it. He was a stickler for detail." The lawyer laughed, a hoarse, barking sound that broke the deep quiet of the room. "He picked out everything from the music to the flowers to his outfit. He wanted to make sure everything was easy on his family, even keeping track of his mementos." He turned to Phillip. "Have you gone through that box he left you yet? I imagine there are some good memories of your dad in there."

Phillip nodded toward Bethany. She was standing beside Rodney, and even though she was wearing five-inch heels, she barely came up to his shoulders. "Bethany's got the box back at my office. I glanced at it. It looks like a lot of old photos and letters." He paused. "We are going to take our time and go through each item he saved."

"He was a good man, and he will surely be missed." Henry rocked back and forth on his feet.

"I do not believe this!" Cindy's voice pierced the air. She marched in at a furious pace, her black dress billowing behind her, stiletto heels not making a sound as she stomped across the thick carpet. "This is unacceptable!" She waved a piece of paper in front of Brian's face.

Brian released Jane's hand and stepped toward Cindy. "Ms. Restin, please tell me what's wrong. How can I help you?"

Jane was impressed by Brian's calm demeanor; she herself

felt as if she had just been attacked by an angry crow.

"This is unacceptable," Cindy repeated as she waved the paper toward Brian again. "I told your incompetent brother that this picture had to be changed." She pointed a manicured nail at the photo of her father on the front of the funeral service announcement. "This picture is terrible! And the Bible verse on the bottom is all wrong!" She drew her lip back in a snarl. "For everything there is a season. Really? Could it be any more predictable than that?"

"Now Cindy." Phillip pulled his hand off Annie and stepped closer to his sister. "We have been through this. Father planned everything himself and we are honoring his wishes by letting him have the service the way he wanted."

"Surely, he didn't want to be remembered like this." Cindy waved the pamphlet in front of Phillip. "Twenty-two years old standing in front of a sign with a cartoon pig?"

Henry reached out and grabbed the pamphlet from Cindy mid-wave. "Er, yes. That is exactly how he wanted to be remembered." He frowned at Cindy and continued in his gravelly voice. "That is a photograph of him at the opening of the tenth restaurant. It was his favorite photo. If you remember, he kept the original framed in his office."

"Maybe it was his favorite, but really, it has no resemblance to him today." Cindy's voice was almost a screech. "He is my father and I will not have him dishonored by an ancient picture with that ridiculous sign. The Restin logo was changed ages ago. We don't use that pig with wings and a halo anymore!"

Rodney winked at Jane. There was the rub, so to speak. Cindy did not want to be associated with smoked pork royalty. Well, too bad for her, Jane thought. There was no chance in the world that anyone in Knoxville would ever think of her as anything but the heir to the Restin Family Barbeque fortune. That is, unless she did something truly awful and shocking.

A Discriminating Death

"I understand your concerns." Henry peered over his glasses at Cindy. "However, this is how your father wanted things and my job is to ensure that his wishes are honored."

Cindy stood speechless for a moment, something that Jane did not believe was actually possible, and then grabbed the pamphlet from Henry and stalked out of the room.

Brian cleared his throat and nodded toward the door. "It's almost time. If the family would like to come with me, we can start the reception line. The mourners have been waiting in the Rose annex until the start of the service. Are you ready?"

Phillip nodded, gave Annie a small smile and followed Brian and Henry from the room. Bethany stood on her tiptoes to whisper in Rodney's ear, and then she too walked toward the door.

When they were finally alone again, Annie let out a huge sigh. "What a terrible woman. I can't believe how she spoke to Brian."

"The old crow had better not do it again, or Jane will be all over her." Rodney glanced at Jane. "I saw you itching to jump into the fight."

"I was not going to jump in! But you're right. I did think she looked like a crow in that get-up. Sort of a cross between Barbie and a crow, if you know what I mean?"

Rodney shuddered theatrically and then turned toward the casket. James Restin had laid still in his eternal repose throughout it all. Really, Jane thought, it was almost as if no one even noticed he was there.

* * *

Jane had attended more funerals than she wanted to recall in her twenty-plus years of life, but this one was unlike anything she had ever seen. Not only were all of Knoxville's movers and shakers there- Jane had seen the Mayor seated beside every member of the County Commission- but it also appeared that every Restin employee had attended. The funeral was standing room only.

Jane leaned against a back wall and tried to keep her eyes open. It was difficult. The lack of sleep and the warm room combined with the low tones of the Presbyterian minister almost did her in. Rodney elbowed her once in the ribs and she straightened up, blinking.

Jane looked at Annie, enrapt watching as Phillip took the podium for the eulogy. Annie had just met Phillip a few days ago, but already Jane could tell that Annie had it bad. Jane couldn't remember the last time a man had made Annie blush.

Jane turned to glance at Rodney, his face tight and pale as he looked through the crowd towards the casket. She wondered if he was thinking about his nightmare. Jane had never attended a police funeral and never wanted to. She guessed it would rival even James Restin's service.

Finally, Jane looked toward the back door. There, standing with his hands clasped behind him, stood Brian. She felt her heart race as she studied his profile. He turned and caught her eye. She smiled and turned her attention back to the service.

Chapter Four

*"In the Tennessee Constitutional Convention of 1843, East Tennesseans succeeded in having the Malungeons officially classified as "free persons of color." This classification was equivalent to declaring them of Negro blood and preventing them from suing or even testifying in court in any case involving a Caucasian."*v

"How did it go last night? Did John and Rodney make up?" Annie whispered as she stripped the thorns off two dozen red roses.

"Stop whispering about me." Rodney walked into the work room and frowned at his friends. "Really, and to think that people say I'm the gossip of this group."

"We're worried about you and John," Jane said. "Annie was just wondering if you guys talked last night." Jane stared at Rodney. He didn't even blink. "And, I was just getting ready to tell her that no, you two most certainly did not talk. Quite the opposite, in fact."

Rodney ran his fingers through his hair and leaned against the doorframe. "Trust me. Last night was not the time for us to hash it out. Not after getting back from that funeral. No way was I in the mood for a heart-to-heart. Besides, I'm still mad at him for lying to me in the first place."

"You're going to have to talk to him sometime," Annie said as she wrapped the large bouquet in green tissue paper. "You and John have been together for a long time and it would be a shame to let something like this come between you."

"Well, I sure won't be talking to him tonight." Rodney took a deep breath. "John's scheduled for a late shift again. It's on the kitchen calendar."

"We're going out tonight anyway, remember?" Jane said. "Brian's meeting us here around five so we can all drive downtown together." She looked over at Annie. "Do you want to come? I bet Bethany needs all the help she can get to fill the audience, and I can guarantee we'll have a great dinner in Market Square."

"Oh no." Annie shook her head. "No, I'm going to go home and have a nice relaxing evening. I'm going to sit in front of the air conditioning vent and read a new book. I'm not even going to make dinner. I think I'm just going to grab a bowl of cold cereal." She put a white ribbon around the bouquet and then set it in an empty bucket. "Running around with you two and then doing that funeral has worn me out. I swear if we didn't have just a half day on Saturdays, I'd never make it."

"Cold cereal and an early bed sound like a great idea." Rodney pulled up a stool and sat down beside Jane. "I'm exhausted too. I haven't had a good night's sleep in two days. Maybe I can call and cancel on Bethany. She won't mind too much."

Jane saw the dark circles around Rodney's eyes. He did look exhausted but she knew that if he was home by himself tonight, he would not be getting any beauty sleep. She briefly allowed herself to indulge in the desire for a night out alone with Brian and then thought of Rodney staring forlornly at the living room walls. "You are going out tonight and that is final." She pointed her finger at him. "You promised Bethany.

A Discriminating Death

What if she gets up to speak and no one is there? You can't let your friend down like that. We are going. Understood?"

Rodney raised his hands in resignation. "Okay, but you're driving. I fully intend to have a couple of drinks tonight, maybe a couple more than a couple."

The front door bells jingled, and Jane glanced at the clock. "That one's all yours, Annie; we don't have anyone till nine."

"Finish your coffee, I'll get it." Rodney slid off the stool.

"Oh, that's okay!" Annie patted her hair and picked up the bouquet of roses at her feet. She smoothed her green apron and rushed toward the front.

"Well, she sure perked up in a hurry." Jane raised an eyebrow at Rodney.

Rodney's eyes narrowed. "Let's just go and find out why, shall we?"

Jane and Rodney walked quietly down the short hallway and peered around the corner into the front reception area. Jane almost laughed out loud when she saw Phillip Restin standing in front of the cash register. He held the roses in one hand while he reached down into a large gift bag.

Rodney elbowed Jane over so that he could get a better view as Phillip pulled an enormous silver vase out of the bag. He pushed the bouquet into the vase, tissue paper and all, and handed it to Annie. "These are for you, to thank you for all of the beautiful work you did for the service. I cannot tell you how much I appreciate you."

"Oh, I can't accept this!" Annie was blushing again as she held the vase in both hands. "Oh, this is too much, really!"

"Please take it." Phillip leaned one hip against the counter. "I noticed all of your antique vases but I didn't think you had one quite like this. It's been in the family for years, but we seldom use it. It needs someone who can appreciate it."

"Oh, please," Rodney breathed heavily into Jane's ear.

Jane scooted back toward the salon room and pulled Rodney with her. Once inside, she shut the door and glared at him. "What do you mean, 'please'? I think it's romantic."

Rodney snarled his lip in disgust. "Really, how much more cliché could the man get?"

"I think it's fabulous. Did you see Annie's face? She thinks it's fabulous too. Oh, I hope he asks her out!"

Rodney opened the door and stuck his head out into the hallway. Jane heard the soft murmur of voices and kept her hand on Rodney's arm as she strained to make out the words.

"Listen," Rodney whispered. "I think that's the front door. Let's go find out what happened."

Jane followed Rodney to the front and found Annie, her face still red, setting the vase on the consultation table by the display window.

"My, my, my." Rodney ran his finger down the side of the vase. "What a gorgeous arrangement. Whoever are they for?"

"Hush, Rodney!" Annie could not keep from smiling as she scolded him.

Jane clapped her hands and grinned. "Please, please tell me that he asked you out."

"He did! We're going out this Monday night. He's sending a car for me. Can you believe it? No one has ever sent a car for me!" Annie's voice rose in a squeal of delight.

"For Heavens sake, the man just buried his ..." Rodney grimaced as Jane stepped on his foot, hard.

The front door bells jingled again, and Jane was relieved to see Rodney's first client enter. She moved her foot off of his shoe and smiled at him. This was the first date that Annie had been out on in a long time and there was no way she was going to let anyone mess it up.

Rodney frowned at her then turned to the door. "Carla, dear! Come on back."

* * *

"You know it isn't good for the environment to just sit here with your car running." Rodney leaned up from the backseat of Jane's used, but new to her, Honda Accord.

"There's no way I'm going to sit in this heat and start sweating like a pig before Brian gets here." Jane glanced at her watch and then looked around the small parking lot of Bloom's. It was ten minutes to five.

"I still can't believe you made me sit in the back seat." Rodney leaned back and crossed his arms. "There's hardly any legroom back here. I'll probably be so cramped up by the time we get downtown that I won't be able to walk from the parking garage to the conference center." His eyes widened. "Oh, I might even get a thrombosis. You know, like on airplanes when you don't get to move around enough and then you get a blood clot in your leg?"

Jane paused to imagine Brian kissing her in some dimly lit restaurant. She was starting to wish she had not been quite so insistent that Rodney get out of the house tonight. "Be serious, Rodney. Now, is Bethany going to meet us at the conference center after her talk or are we going to meet her in Market Square?"

"She's going to meet us at Tomato Head at seven. She's got reservations for the four of us. It appears that you are the only one that has a boyfriend coming along tonight."

"Rodney." Jane looked at him in the rearview mirror. His face was pinched and cross. "You had better make up with John, and I mean soon. You being miserable is making me miserable too."

"Hey," Rodney smirked, "that would be a great name for the salon. 'Misery and Company.' What do you think?"

Jane looked up and saw Brian's black Audi pull into Bloom's parking lot. "Wait, here he is." She turned quickly to Rodney and glared. "Now be nice. Promise?"

"I promise," Rodney sighed. "Really, Jane, you take all the fun out of being crabby."

Jane watched Brian lock his car and walk toward her. A

wave of heat swept in as he opened the passenger door. He leaned close to her and she closed her eyes, waiting for the kiss.

"Ahem!" Rodney cleared his throat loudly.

Brian jumped a little and winked at Jane.

"Hey Brian, I had no idea you were interested in family history." Rodney smiled wickedly.

"Oh, I've kind of inherited the interest." Brian laughed as he buckled his seat belt. "I had an aunt who started keeping track of our lines, and now it's up to me." He looked at Jane and smiled. "Also, I figured this was my best chance to see Jane this weekend, other than at work of course. You two could be headed to a monster truck rally or an impressionist dance performance and I would've begged to tag along."

Jane grinned all the way downtown.

* * *

They had no trouble parking. The city offered free parking in all of the downtown garages to encourage visitors during the weekends. Their only problem was trying to squeeze through the packed crowds mingling in the conference center lobby.

"Are all these people here for family history stuff?" Rodney asked. He stepped to one side as several people wearing bright yellow shirts proudly proclaiming 'Roberson Family' shuffled past.

"It's a bigger deal than I thought," Jane admitted. "Where's Bethany going to be? What conference room?"

"She said she'd be in the basement. The Melungeon talks are going to be where they set up the Fantasy of Trees."

Jane nodded. Everyone was familiar with the Fantasy of Trees. It was a Christmas tradition in Knoxville. Businesses and floral designers, churches, schools, social clubs and Boy Scout groups all donated decorated artificial trees, wreaths or elaborate gingerbread houses. A carousel was brought indoors

A Discriminating Death

and craft stations were set up for the kids. All proceeds went to the Children's Hospital. Bloom's had participated for the last three years, and Rodney and Jane looked forward to helping Annie start designing their tree early each September.

"Okay, into the fray!" Rodney tucked his head down and started to gently push his way toward the stairs. Jane felt as though electricity poured through her as Brian grabbed her hand and followed Rodney.

It took fifteen minutes, four people stepping on Jane's feet, and Rodney taking two elbows to the ribs before they finally entered the conference room. It was packed.

"I had no idea that Bethany could draw a crowd like this," Jane said. "I thought this was going to be a little talk, maybe twenty people max!"

"I'm surprised too." Rodney looked suitably impressed. "She told me she published a couple of articles about the Melungeons, but I didn't think it was anything this big."

"Look. There are a few seats open over there." Brian pointed to the far left side of the room. Rodney quickly pushed his way over and they were able to sit together at the end of a row. They couldn't really see the stage very well, but Jane didn't mind. She could feel Brian's thigh press up against her leg and she knew she would be able to think of little else.

The lights dimmed and the room grew quiet. "Here she comes." Rodney's voice was more animated than Jane had heard it all day. She no longer regretted forcing him out of the house. That is, as long as he continued to behave himself for the rest of the evening.

Bethany was so short that she needed to step up onto a wooden box placed behind the podium. She stacked her papers and then cleared her throat once. The sound echoed around the room and the audience grew quiet.

"First of all, thank you for coming tonight. My name is Bethany Collins, and I am a Melungeon."

Loud whoops of encouragement and shrill whistles startled Jane.

Bethany laughed and held up her hands. "I can hear that there are a lot of Melungeons in the crowd tonight! I hope all of you make sure to check the 'other' box on your census forms and write in Melungeon. We've been discounted and hidden for too long. Now, with the help of the latest advancements in DNA research, we finally have the chance to tell the story of our proud heritage."

Jane settled back into her chair, this time focusing on the feeling of Brian's shoulder touching her shoulder. The talk was looking as if it were going to be interesting and there wasn't any place she'd rather be.

"Now, I am sure that most of us know the various theories about the history of the Melungeons; but just in case there are some newcomers in the crowd, I'd like to give a little background information.

"The theories about the origins of the Melungeons range from the possible to the ridiculous and everything in between. We have been told that we are the descendants of the Lost Colony of Roanoke, descendants of the lost tribe of Israel, the spawn of the devil and his Indian wife, a mix of Indian and freed blacks, descendants of Spanish soldiers brought here by Juan Pardo in 1566, and descendants of Turkish and Moroccan settlers. Regardless of the stories floating around them, the group of people called Melungeons consistently reported that they were Portuguese. Now, maybe they were and maybe they weren't, but for many years being considered Portuguese was certainly safer than being considered colored.

"No one knows when Melungeons were first discovered, but Governor John Sevier came across a large group of them here in Tennessee around two hundred and fifty years ago. Now the Scotch-Irish...and how many of you grew up believing you were Scotch-Irish?" Bethany paused while laughter filled the room. Jane was confused. She'd always been told that she was Scotch-Irish and she didn't see anything funny about

A Discriminating Death

that at all.

Bethany took a sip of water and continued. "Now the Scotch-Irish and the English settlers who came here expected to find land free of inhabitants, other than those pesky Indians, that is. Well, what do they find but a large group of mostly dark-skinned, blue-eyed people living on the fertile bottom lands? What to do with these earliest settlers? Why, label them as 'Free Persons of Color', of course."

Bethany shook her head sadly. "It was a strategic move. If you were a Free Person of Color, you could not own land, could not vote, could not get an education in the public schools and absolutely could not marry a so-called 'white' person. At first the Melungeons fought back and then they moved back, farther and farther into the mountains, giving up their prosperous farms and hoping to be left alone.

"As of now, we cannot state with certainty the specific origin of the Melungeons. I personally believe the theory presented by the father of Melungeon research, Brent Kennedy. I think he's correct in his view that Sir Francis Drake dropped off a lot of South American Muslims just off the coast of present-day North Carolina. He had planned on dropping them off in Cuba to help confound the Spanish, but bad weather steered his ships toward Roanoke Island. The idea that this population intermarried with local Native Americans, is confirmed, for me at least, by the similarities in so many Turkish and Native American words and customs."

She pressed a button and a large PowerPoint display came on behind her showing two columns of words. "Now, we don't know exactly where the name of our great state of Tennessee came from, but it sure sounds like the Turkish word 'tenasuh' which means 'a place where souls move about.' Not a bad name, considering that the Native American word 'Kentucky' is supposed to mean 'bloody ground,' which sounds suspiciously like the Turkish word 'kan tok,' which translates into 'full of blood.'"

Jane was shocked. She never knew any of this. She sure hadn't learned it in her high school history classes.

"My favorite state name has to be Alabama." Bethany laughed into the microphone. "Think about the Turkish words 'Alla bamya' during the next UT-Bama game and remember that the translation is 'God's cemetery.'"

She pressed another button and two black- and-white photos appeared. One was obviously a dark-skinned Middle Eastern man standing beside a tent. The other man looked identical except for his dirty overalls and straw hat. He was seated on a cane chair beside a log cabin door.

"This first picture was in National Geographic. It is a picture of a Moorish Berber. The second picture is of my great-grandfather, William Collins." She paused and looked around the room. "Now, I know that many of you are familiar with the work of the infamous Dr. Plecker in Virginia."

Boos and hisses erupted from the room. Jane looked at Brian who shrugged. Rodney just looked confused.

"Now, the Plecker laws, especially the 1924 Racial Integrity Act, set our people back generations. It is my belief that we are just now starting to recover from the harm that man caused. We were labeled as colored in 1924, a mere nine years after the Ku Klux Klan movement regained momentum. We lived in fear and shame. As long as we were considered to have one drop of colored blood, local clerks would deny marriage licenses to Melungeons attempting to marry a 'white' person. Our children were not allowed to attend 'white' schools, and most Melungeons rebelled at the thought of sending their children to the 'colored' schools. In their minds, that would only cement the fact they're 'colored,' and therefore powerless in their fight to be relabeled as Portuguese or Indian. The less power we had, the poorer we grew and the poorer we grew, the less power we had. To this day, it astounds me to think that the Racial Discrimination Act was not off Virginia's law books until 1971. By that time, we had lost

A Discriminating Death

the most precious thing of all, our sense of pride in our history. We hid or destroyed our family photos and stories. We lied to our children about their heritage.

"I know that your presence here today means that you are interested in your heritage, maybe even proud of it. But I also know that you might very well have a beloved granny or great-aunt back home who grew up in the time when Melungeons were hated and feared. This elderly relative may very well strip your hide if she knew that you were running around telling everyone that your family is Melungeon instead of Cherokee or Scotch-Irish. Our relatives only want the best for us. They well know the price they paid for being different, and they only want to spare us that pain. Now is the time to gently assure them that they have a lot to be proud of. Now is the time to recognize and celebrate their history of struggle and dignity."

Jane leaned forward in her seat. The room was humming with excited murmurs.

"The Melungeon Mountain Heritage Foundation is conducting a DNA analysis of the Melungeons in our area. It is vital that everyone participate. The larger the sample population we can collect, the greater the truth that will be revealed. Not only will we learn how we are connected to each other, but we will be able to trace maternal DNA back to our origins. The testing is free to all participants, but a donation would greatly be appreciated. Please pick up a form and collection kit at the tables set up in the main lobby. Please also pick up a family history questionnaire and list of common Melungeon surnames to help you with your own family research."

Bethany took another sip of water and carefully placed the glass back on the podium. "Are there any questions?"

About half the audience raised their arms and started waving. Jane kept her hands down even though she had a question, a big one. Why had she never heard of any of this before?

"Can I have the goat cheese sandwich with a side of tahini, please? Oh, and I'm positively dying for a bottle of Blue Moon ale." Rodney folded his menu and handed it to the waiter.

"That sounds good. I think I'll take the same." Brian looked at Jane. "What are you in the mood for?"

"I'm going to stick with the pizza. Just cheese and mushroom please." Jane handed the waiter her menu. "And I'll take an ice water." She looked at Rodney. "I promised I'd drive tonight."

Bethany did not even glance at her menu. "I'll take the tofu bowl special please, and an ice water too."

As the waiter left to turn in their orders, Rodney looked at Bethany seated beside him. "I am so impressed with you! I always knew you were smart, but this was something else. You had quite a crowd out there."

"I'm impressed too," Jane agreed. "I hate to admit it, but I had never heard of the Melungeons before tonight."

"I have," Brian said. "Not in a positive way, but I have heard of them."

"It's amazing isn't it?" Bethany smiled. "A whole separate people, a whole separate culture, here in our backyard. The Melungeons settled in Newman's Ridge in Hancock County. That's just a couple of hours away from us."

Jane flipped through the handouts that she had picked up in the lobby after Bethany's talk. "I think that I might have some Melungeon roots. I mean, my mother's side of the family includes some Shephards, Garlands and even a Campbell." She frowned. "The Campbell connection was always what made mom tell us we were Scotch-Irish. Isn't Campbell a Scottish clan?"

Bethany moved her silverware out of the way as the waiter set their drinks down in front of them. "Well, family history isn't an exact science. That's why we're so glad to be able to

A Discriminating Death

trace the maternal DNA of our participants. You sound like you'd qualify. Why don't you do a cheek swab and see if you are related to the Scotch-Irish you've been told about?"

"I have some of these names too," Rodney said thoughtfully as he sipped his beer. "How many Melungeons do you think there are?"

"Who knows?" Bethany shrugged. "More and more are coming out of the closet every day."

"I was shocked by the Plecker laws you spoke about," Brian said. "I know that discrimination happened, but I guess I automatically assumed the racial laws just applied to African Americans. When it comes to prejudice against Native Americans, all I learned about in school was the infamous Trail of Tears. I never learned one thing about discrimination against Melungeons."

"I know," Bethany said. "The Melungeons were not only left out of society, they were left out of our history books. Most of them just tucked their heads down and kept a low profile. Some of them, the blonde–hair, blued-eyed Melungeons who could pass for white, up and left the area to disappear into larger cities."

Rodney took a large drink and snorted. "Discrimination is just a part of this weary old life. The history books have been biased against gays, blacks, and women for ages. At least some of the Melungeons could pass for white. They could kind of hide in plain sight, like some gay gentlemen I know who have not yet told their families the truth."

"Well, being a Melungeon back in the day would be a little bit different than being gay," Brian laughed. "Think about it. The whole family would be Melungeon, right? So there'd be no hiding the truth from them. A homosexual person can choose to keep his secrets from his family and everyone else."

"What a terrible choice those families had to make," Bethany sighed. "Just imagine if you were a poor, dark-skinned Melungeon living back in the ridges of East Tennessee and you happened to have blonde-haired, blue-eyed children who could pass. Wouldn't you want them to move to somewhere they weren't known? They could change their names and start fresh, but only at the cost of denying their true history."

"I don't think that would be worth it," Jane said. "To completely cut yourself off from the only life you knew just so you could pass as white?"

"I bet it was worth it for a lot of people." Rodney took another drink. "The chance to be accepted in society and have your children find a place in the world where they could get an education, own property, and vote? Come on, who wouldn't do it?"

"But wait," Jane said. "Let's say these blonde Melungeons did sneak off and start over and marry another 'white' person. Couldn't their kids still come out dark-skinned?"

"Oh yes, or worse, they could have six fingers," Bethany laughed. "Ah, well, we are all a blend, aren't we? Mutts, every one of us."

"Can you imagine having such a big secret from your spouse? How can people be in relationships without the truth?" Rodney absently folded a napkin into squares.

"Now wait." Jane glanced at Rodney and then looked back at Bethany. "What does having six fingers have to do with anything?" Brian put his arm around Jane's chair and leaned closer toward the table. Jane could feel her blood rush to her head as his arm pressed against her back.

"Oh, that's an old wives tale about Melungeons. Supposedly, you could tell someone was a Melungeon because they had six fingers on one hand." Bethany reached down and picked up her briefcase from under the table. "Actually, there was some truth to it. Not every Melungeon had six fingers of course, but the genetic trait is more prevalent in that population."

She pulled out a book and started to flip through it. "There are some good pictures of Melungeons in here, both dark-skinned and lighter. In one of the chapters, there's a photo of an older Melungeon gentleman with six fingers on his left hand."

Jane thought back to her family history of names. "Do you have any books you'd recommend to help me get started with researching my family?"

"You can borrow this one. It's one of my favorites." Bethany closed it and handed the book across the table just as the waiter appeared.

"Thanks. I'll make sure and get it back to you at your next appointment." Jane reached for the paperback just as Rodney picked it up.

"Can I take a look at that?" He flipped through the pages as the waiter cleared room for their plates.

"Careful now, these are hot." The waiter set several plates down in front of them.

"There's no way you can eat all of that by yourself." Rodney flashed Jane a fake smile as he eyed her pizza. "Why don't you let me help you out?"

"Don't even think about it."

"What I am really thinking about is another beer." Rodney waved his empty glass at the waiter and placed the book in his lap. "Thanks."

Bethany closed her eyes as she took a bite. "Oh, I'm hungry. I missed lunch today because I got stuck at the office."

"You have to work Saturdays?" Brian asked.

"Not usually, but we missed a lot of our regular work this week, what with the funeral preparations and all, not to mention Phillip's new project." Bethany quickly looked around the restaurant and then lowered her voice. "Phillip is going to launch a campaign for governor next year. Isn't that exciting? His dad always wanted him to run the family business; but now that he's passed, Phillip is ready to go after what he really wants. He's going to make a formal announcement on Monday morning."

Jane thought that Phillip might as well skip the press release. She'd seen the glimmer in Rodney's eyes as he learned a fresh piece of "social information," his term for gossip, and Jane was well aware the news would be spread far and wide before Monday came.

"That is interesting." Rodney almost purred. "He'll need every cent he can get from the resort development if he's going to fund his campaign. Will you go to Nashville with him?"

"Who knows? The election is over a year away, there's plenty of time to think about my options. It may be time for me to make a fresh start too."

"Has he chosen a running mate yet?" Rodney's voice was full of innocent curiosity.

Jane decided it was time to change the subject. "How is Phillip doing after the funeral? Is he holding up okay?"

"As well as can be expected," Bethany put down her fork. "I really think James' death was a kind of relief. It was hard on Phillip to see his dad in such a debilitated state for so many months and not be able to do anything to help him. Right now, Phillip also has to deal with the family graveyard being dug up and moved to a private cemetery in West Knoxville. The development committee decided that a graveyard in the resort would not be a draw for customers. They've had to knock down trees and build a road wide enough for the trucks to get through to the cemetery. It's almost finished and they'll start moving graves in a couple of weeks. Phillip didn't actually know anyone buried there, but it still has to be strange for him to have all of his relatives dug up so soon after burying his dad. Once the move is over and they have a memorial service at the new site, I think things will be easier for everyone."

"I can't imagine," Jane whispered.

"I was hoping to find something to do as a tribute to honor Phillip's family. At first I thought about a starting a grant or planting a tree in James' honor, but now I have a better idea. I'm going to need your help, though," Bethany said.

"What do you mean?" Rodney asked as the waiter placed another cold beer in front of him.

"This morning I started sorting that big box from the lawyer's office. So far, it's mostly old letters and documents from the family. I was thinking that I could put together a short family tree, kind of an ornate hand-drawn document and I was hoping that Grace could dry some flowers from the funeral and put them in the frame. How long does it take her to get the flowers pressed?"

"I think it takes a couple of weeks," Rodney said. "I know that Annie still has some of the yellow roses left over from the arrangements. I could get Grace to go ahead and get started on them before they lose any color. How many do you think you'll need?"

"I'm not sure." Bethany shrugged. "I can draw up a rough sketch of the size of the tree I am thinking of and mail it to you. It will take me a while to get all of the names and dates verified, but Grace can at least play around with the layout while we wait."

Jane leaned forward. "Rodney can do the calligraphy. He has fabulous penmanship. He's doing Grace's wedding invitations and he's done almost all of the framed pieces Grace puts together."

"You did the one by the front door, right?"

Rodney waved his hand as if it were nothing. "That one's mine. There's nothing to it. I'd be happy to sketch out a small family tree for you. How about three generations back? That would put James's name right on the trunk."

"That would be perfect. Phillip will love it."

"Should I do two? One for Cindy?"

Bethany paused, a small frown forming on her face. "Oh, I don't think so. Cindy and I don't exactly get along. I very much doubt she wants a present from me."

Jane caught Brian's eye and smiled. She wondered how often Bethany had to deal with Cindy. She herself had only seen the woman twice and each time had been a decidedly unpleasant experience.

"What happened?" Rodney asked. "You get along with everyone."

Bethany looked at him. "I stopped getting along with Cindy the moment I walked into my boyfriend's office and found her draped half-naked across his desk."

"No!" Rodney put his hand over his mouth. "She didn't."

"She did. She'd never even given Garret a second glance until she saw us together at a company picnic. Cindy is the type of woman who only wants what someone else has. Once I dumped him, she did too."

"She's even worse than I thought," Jane said. "How could you have stayed working there after that?"

"I like my job, and I like Phillip." Bethany shrugged. "He's always been good to me and there was no way I was going to let Cindy take everything away from me. Phillip's sweet. Once he heard about the incident, he quietly arranged for Garret to take a traveling position. The way I figure it, Cindy actually did me a favor. I'm glad I found out Garret was such a jerk before I got too serious with him. Really, I got over it much faster than Cindy has. She can barely stand to be in the same room with me. But, she's hardly ever in the office, so I don't have to see her very much."

"I don't know any faithful men," Rodney said. "Other than me, of course."

"At least Phillip helped get Garret out of the office," Brian said. "He must realize how lucky he is to have you. Does he know about your research? Is he interested in his family history?"

"He knows I serve on the Melungeon Mountain Heritage Foundation, but he's much more interested in the next political trend than in anything that happened two hundred years ago."

"How did you get interested in Melungeon research?"

A Discriminating Death

Brian asked.

Jane saw Rodney's eyes light back up when Bethany mentioned politics. She resisted the urge to give him a warning kick under the table.

"I took a genealogy class in college. Actually, it was right after Rodney dumped me," Bethany laughed.

"Hey now, I never dumped you! I just told you that that I had a crush on Chad."

"I know, I know." Bethany patted him on the arm. "You broke my heart without trying, but you have made it up to me by fixing my hair all these years, so I think we can call it even." She looked back across the table. "Anyway, I took this class and started to suspect the things my grandmother had told me were not quite the truth. Unfortunately, when I confronted her about it, she grew angry. When I told her that I thought we were Melungeons, she didn't talk to me ever again. She actually died before being willing to speak with me about our background."

"Oh, that's just terrible," Jane said.

"It was terrible," Bethany agreed. "After her funeral, I was more determined than ever to find out the truth. I joined the Heritage Foundation and now, two years and three research articles later, I'm one of their speakers."

"You did a great job." Brian smiled at Bethany. Jane ignored the sharp little pang of jealousy that stabbed at her.

Rodney dipped half of his sandwich into the tahini sauce. "So, if I can prove I'm Melungeon, will I get a minority rate on my business loan? Apparently being gay isn't enough, and it is going to cost a lot of money to open 'Rodney and Friends Hair Emporium.'"

Chapter Five

"The saints and hobgoblins! The witch of Endor calling dead Saul from the sepulchral darkness would have calked her ears and fled forever at the sight of this living, breathing Malungeon witch... She was small, scant, raw-boned, sharp-ankled, barefoot, short frock literally hanging from the knee in rags. A dark jacket with great yellow patches on either breast,
   sleeves torn away above the elbow, black hair burnt to an unfashionable auburn long ago, and a corncob pipe wedged between the toothless gums... I never saw an uglier human creature, or one more gross-looking and unattractive. [vi]

"How did it go last night?" John was seated in the kitchen, the early morning light clearly showing the fatigue that etched his face.

Jane helped herself to a cup of coffee and sat across from him.

"Did Rodney say anything about me?" John propped his head in his hands. "Did you talk about me at all?"

"Not really, no." Jane felt sorry for John. She felt sorry for Rodney too.

"I just don't know what I'm going to do, Jane. I can't

imagine life without Rodney. I know he can drive a person insane, but oh, I do love him."

John's expression went blank as Rodney walked into the kitchen. Zeke, feeling the tension in the air, left his food bowl and slipped under Jane's chair.

Jane sipped her coffee and watched Rodney pour a bowl of Cheerios. This was the first time that he and John had been in the same room since their fight. She glanced at John, who was staring intently into his coffee cup. So far, neither of them had started shouting obscenities at each other. Jane felt that was progress of a sort.

Rodney sat down at the table and scooted his chair so that he was turned away from John. "Good morning, Jane. I hope you slept well."

Jane had heard Rodney cry out again last night. She knew that he hadn't slept well at all. "I slept fine, but I did have the strangest dream about Deborah. She was doing our family history research and discovered that we were related to this family of skunks that lived under our front porch when we were growing up."

Rodney grinned at her. "I imagine Deborah would not be happy about that."

"Ah, no. Even in the dream, she was pretty particular about things." Jane shouldn't have worried about being diplomatic; Rodney and John both knew how bossy her older sister could be. "I do think that I'm going to send her the questionnaire from last night, just in case she knows something I don't."

"Honey, there's no chance that Deborah is going to know more about your family history than you do, but I guess it can't hurt to start there. She's all you've got for now."

Rodney was right. Deborah was all the family Jane had. Their mother had been killed in a car wreck a few weeks after Jane finished high school. Deborah was already enrolled in college and strongly encouraged Jane to take the inheritance and start at UT in the fall, but Jane just wasn't ready. In the end, Deborah took the life insurance money and Jane took the house on Kingston Pike, the house that was currently under renovation as new living quarters and a salon.

Deborah had graduated, married, and moved to Florida. She and Jane did try to stay in touch. They'd talk on the phone a couple of times a month, and Deborah would forward Jane joke emails, but that was about the extent of their relationship. They were just two very different people.

Rodney pointed at Jane with his spoon, dripping milk on the kitchen table. "Don't worry about Deborah. That book Bethany gave us last night has a whole chapter on how to start your research. I can help you with all of the online stuff. I'm going to check mine out too. I'm sure I have a couple of Melungeon surnames on my maternal grandmother's side."

John stood up and poured another cup of coffee. Jane tried to catch his eye, but he refused to look at her or Rodney.

A loud thud came from the foyer as the newspaper hit the front door. The paperboy had quite an arm. Jane had long since given up going outside before the paper came. She never wanted to be pelted with the Sunday edition.

Rodney shot up out of his chair. "I'll get it."

John sat back down and nodded once at Jane. She smiled back at him. They both knew that Rodney only wanted to grab the paper to keep their nosy neighbor Bill from seeing John. Rodney was convinced that the retired military man would peer out his curtains until John came out to pick up the paper, check the morning's mail, or take out the trash. Then, Bill would head out his door and 'accidentally' run into John. John always stopped and talked to Bill for a good four or five minutes each time. Jane wasn't sure if it was because he didn't want to hurt Bill's feelings or if it was because he liked to rile Rodney. She thought it was a good omen that Rodney was still jealous.

Zeke crept out from under the chair and jumped up onto

Jane's lap. She petted him slowly and listened to his throaty purr. Jane shifted her weight slightly to get more comfortable. Despite the veterinarian-ordered diet, Zeke still remained a hefty cat.

"What the hell is this?" Rodney stood in the doorway, holding the paper in front of him.

"Let me see it." John started to stand up.

"Wait," Rodney growled. John lowered himself back down into his chair. The kitchen was silent as Rodney continued reading.

Finally Rodney folded the paper. Zeke jumped off Jane's lap and returned to his hiding spot under her chair as Rodney approached. "Is this, or is this not, the skank that we saw Thursday night?"

"What?" Jane asked as Rodney pushed the paper into her hands. One large photograph dominated the front page; without a doubt it was the spiky-haired woman that John had kissed. She was holding a sign and yelling, her mouth was open and Jane could see the veins standing out on her neck. "What is this about?"

"Read the article," Rodney spat. "It's quite an education as to what John has been up to lately."

John sat still while Jane scanned the article. Rodney stood beside her, purposely refusing to look in John's direction.

At first, the news did not seem that bad. Some environmental activist group was protesting a development project downtown. Jane wasn't too alarmed until she read that the group was connected with some seriously escalating threats of violence and vandalism. There were rumors that linked them to several fires, sabotaged machinery, and stolen equipment on construction sites, but no hard evidence had been found.

"Are you really involved with these people?" Jane pushed the paper across the table.

John glanced down at the photograph. "Yes, I am. The group is called SON. It stands for Save Our Nature, but they

A Discriminating Death

are not your run of the mill earth-loving hippie environmentalists." John looked at Rodney who was still ignoring him. "This is serious, Rodney. You can't talk to anyone about this, no one. Do you understand? Not only would we get in real trouble with the department, but we could all be in real danger if they find out I'm a cop. I want you to stay completely away from this."

Rodney spun around, and Jane flinched. She could feel the anger radiating off of him. "You want me to stay completely away from them? Well, I want *you* to stay completely away from them."

"This is my job, Rodney. This is what I do for a living. You know this."

"Oh, I know a lot of things. I know that I don't want to lie in bed at night and wonder if you are out with a group of people who think that setting fires is a reasonable idea. I know that I don't want to have any more nightmares about attending your funeral. I know that I don't want to live like this any more."

Jane wished she could disappear.

"Not everything is about what you want, Rodney. I want some things too. Now, stop acting like a spoiled child and try to see the bigger picture here. I'm doing important work. I'm helping to ensure that these people don't keep breaking the law and endangering lives."

"Oh, yes, John, the rescuer." Rodney put his hands on the table and leaned in toward John. "John, the hero, doing his important work. You must protect the public, but what about your relationship? You lied to me and went behind my back to take an assignment because you were too scared to tell me the truth. Some brave hero you are. People think I am the drama queen, but you thrive on it, don't you? Big bad John needs to do exciting things and be needed by everyone. You don't care about my feelings at all, not as long as you get what you want."

John's eyes flashed as he stood up. Jane shrank back in her chair. "You are going to accuse me of being the selfish one? You are the one that wants me to change my job, change my whole life. Of course I lied to you! I was relieved that I was under orders to keep it a secret because I dreaded telling you I was back on duty. I knew that you would react just like this. I knew you wouldn't see reason. I can't win with you, Rodney. Everything I do is wrong."

"Oh, so it's my fault that you lied to me? It's my fault that you snuck around behind my back?" Rodney pressed his hand against his chest. "Not everything you do is wrong, John, just everything lately. Do not speak to me again until you are ready to apologize."

Rodney stormed out of the kitchen. Jane jumped when he slammed the bedroom door.

Chapter Six

"These folks...are indeed America's outcasts. They, more than any other class, might properly be called 'forgotten men.'"[vii]

Even at nine o'clock in the morning, the temperature inside Jane's car was well over one hundred. Jane eased herself in, thankful that she had not bought the upgraded model with leather seats. She was also thankful to be getting out of the house. Yesterday had been almost unbearable. She could not remember a more miserable Sunday afternoon. John and Rodney both stomped around, sulking and angry and refusing to talk to each other or to her. She finally had retreated with Zeke to the guest bedroom where she read books all afternoon. She only ventured out once to make a peanut butter and honey sandwich for dinner and then had scurried back to her room to eat in silence.

She turned the air-conditioning on full blast and headed west on Kingston Pike. She wished that Rodney had agreed to come with her to check out the salon's progress this morning. Not only did she want him at the construction site with her to buffer her conversation with their site supervisor, Mark, she also felt bad about leaving him all alone in the house. John's sheets had been folded at the end of the sofa when she got up; he must have chosen to leave for work early to avoid any chance of further confrontation. Rodney promised her that he'd be fine alone, that he was going to do some more research online. Jane didn't ask if he was researching his family tree or the SON group. She wasn't sure she wanted to know. He did agree to meet up at Bloom's at noon. Jane promised to grab some more paint samples from Home Depot and then pick up lunch for everyone.

Just as her car was finally cooling off, she pulled into her driveway and parked on the grass beside the carport. There were trucks parked everywhere and workmen scurrying about, seemingly oblivious to the heat.

Jane climbed out of her car and fanned herself with one hand as she looked for signs of progress. She heard the squeal of a saw and watched as two Hispanic men dressed in long-sleeved shirts cut pieces of beige tile.

"Howdy, Jane!" Mark Hammond took off his cap and wiped his brow as he walked up to her. "Have you come to make sure we're still workin'?"

Jane gritted her teeth and smiled at him. She and Rodney had contracted with Hammond Construction Company to repair the house and build the shop. During the design phase they had dealt with Jeff Hammond. Jane liked him well enough, but she wasn't so sure about his brother Mark. Mark was the man in the field and Jane had to admit that he was almost always on site whenever she stopped by. He just rubbed her the wrong way. Rodney swore it was because Mark had called her 'Sweetie' once when she was asking about a code compliance. That had irritated her, but there was more to her distaste for the man than his good old boy sexism.

She nodded toward the men working the wet saw. "I thought the tile was supposed to be in by the weekend. Did you run into any problems?"

Mark winked at her, and Jane tried not to curl her lip in

A Discriminating Death

disgust. "Yep, we had a couple of fellows come up with Friday night fever."

Jane felt the sweat start to form on the back of her neck. "Mark, why would high school football have anything to do with missing work?"

Mark laughed out loud, a harsh sound that carried over the noise of the saw. Jane noticed that the workers quickly glanced at Mark before they returned to their jobs. "These boys get paid on Friday, and half of them are too hung-over to come in to work on Saturday. Now, we've been talking to them about their idea of work ethics, but I swear it's like talking to a dog." Mark shook his head. "Now honey, you don't have to worry about it. I'm on top of it, and I give you my solemn word that the tile will be finished by tomorrow. Now, did you and your partner ever make a decision on the wall paint?"

"Not yet, no." Jane frowned and wished again that Rodney had come over with her; he would know exactly what to say. She was most certainly not Mark's 'honey,' and if he said it one more time, she was going to have to call him out on it. "We should have something finalized by this afternoon."

"Call me when you do and we can have the walls finished this week too. Yep, this place is really shaping up."

Jane hoped that was true. The way things were going, Rodney would have to move in with her before too long. "Is it okay if I go take a look at the progress?" Jane asked.

"Sure, sure. Help yourself."

Jane walked behind the house, glad to be free of Mark's company. She had to be careful where she stepped. The yard was totally destroyed. The fire hadn't helped the lawn, but the greatest damage was done by the construction itself. Fortunately, the plans called for landscaping after the building was complete. She envisioned the house with the addition, just as she had seen drawn on the architect sketches a thousand times. It was hard to believe that she and Rodney were so close to realizing their dream of owning their own shop. Just a couple of more months and everything would be perfect.

She watched a young worker unwrapping boxes behind the house. She carefully picked her way through the stacks of discarded packaging material to inspect what he was doing.

"Hello." The wiry Hispanic man nodded at Jane.

She knew he didn't speak much English. Most of the workers didn't. She sure didn't know much Spanish. Two years of French in high school had done nothing for her. She always felt self-conscious around the workers, way too embarrassed to try to speak the few words of Spanish that she did know. Jane resorted to smiling and pointing to the box.

The worker smiled back as he pulled away some plastic wrapping and unveiled the bowl of a pedestal sink. Jane was thrilled it had finally arrived. Rodney had thrown a fit and insisted on a very specific design, and Home Depot had to special order it for them. Jane thought a sink was a sink, but according to Rodney, nothing could be further from the truth. She wished he was as certain about wall colors or a salon name as he was about plumbing.

She smiled to the worker again and started walking to the far side of the house where the majority of the fire damage had occurred. It was reassuring to see the exterior walls standing, rebuilt and strong.

She turned the corner and was startled to see Mark holding an older Hispanic man up by his shirt collar.

Mark was leaning in close and sputtering in rage. "Comprende? This comes out of your pay check you stupid spic. Do you know how much you've cost us?"

"Excuse me!" Jane shouted as she hurried around piles of tile and wood. "What's going on here?"

Mark released his grip on the man's shirt and pushed him backward. The older worker looked down at his feet and quickly walked back toward the wet saw.

Mark grabbed Jane's arm and pulled her along as he followed the worker. He leaned down and spoke loudly into her

A Discriminating Death

ear. "Honey, you just have to excuse me for losing my temper like that, but I am madder than a hornet. That idiot wet back has ruined almost half of your tile. He used the wrong saw blade and chipped every single piece he's cut."

Jane saw the man flinch at the sound of Mark's voice. "Now don't you worry 'bout nothin'. He understands he has to pay back every cent of the damage he's done." Mark raised his voice and yelled toward the man. Other workers stepped back out of the range of his anger and looked down the ground. "It'll take you weeks, Pedro, but you are going to repay every single penny! No more money to send back to your kin in Ol' Mehico —eh?"

"Now wait a minute!" Jane pulled her arm out of Mark's grasp. "You have no right to talk to him that way. I'm sure we can work this out and fix the tile problem. Now you listen and you listen good - this is my property, and I will not tolerate you speaking to your workers like that."

Mark narrowed his eyes and glared at her. Jane fought the impulse to look away.

"Missy, you have no idea how a construction project is run. You don't know what it takes to get this lazy bunch of illiterates to work, so you just back off and leave me to my job. You go fix hair, and I'll take care of this."

"Get off of my property," Jane spoke quietly. "You're fired."

"You can't fire me!" Mark's eyes widened. "We have a contract."

"I have a contract with your company, but I know I didn't sign anything that said you'd have to be the on-site supervisor. You and Jeff will just have to find somebody else to finish up here, because if you don't leave my property in five minutes, I am going to call the police. Also, I am not your damn 'honey', got it?"

Mark sneered at her. "You are going to regret this." He turned and barked at the workers. "Vamanos! Now! Everyone leave!"

Jane watched in amazement as all of the men, including the older worker by the wet saw, quietly gathered their equipment. They kept their heads down and never looked at her. They threw their tools in the backs of their trucks, climbed into the cabs and then silently left.

Mark was the last to go. He didn't look back as he pulled out of the driveway.

* * *

Jane spent the next hour in Home Depot, going over tile selections again and again. She figured she needed a back up plan in case they couldn't get more of the original. She also thought they would need more paint samples if they were going to change the floors. She picked out several neutrals and wondered what else she could do to delay going to Bloom's.

She glanced at her watch. It was almost eleven. She might as well order lunch and then go face Rodney. She didn't know how she was going to explain to him that she had single-handedly shut down work for the foreseeable future. His week had been bad enough, he didn't need this setback.

She called Ruby Tuesdays and placed an order for pick-up before she left the air-conditioning of the home store. She ducked her head and walked out into the hot parking lot. Jane hated August. Well, February and August to be exact. Each month was the tail end of nasty weather. Thankfully, autumn was just around the corner, and soon the leaves would start changing. Jane wondered if Deborah ever missed the change of seasons. It would be nice to be in Florida from Christmas to Easter, but she could never imagine actually moving away from Tennessee.

She drove to the restaurant and parked in the spot for pick-up orders. Within two minutes, a waitress carrying a large bag knocked on her window. Jane paid the bill and then drove as slowly as possible to the floral shop.

All too soon, Jane was standing on Bloom's front porch. There was no more putting off the inevitable. The bells jingled as she opened the door. "Annie? Rodney?"

"Hey Jane!" Grace stood up from behind the front counter.

"Grace! You scared me to death!" Jane's heart was racing. "I didn't know you'd be back today." Jane held up the bag in her hand. "Oh no, I just picked up lunch and didn't get you anything."

"She can have half of mine." Annie walked out from the work room carrying a display of pink carnations in a porcelain baby carriage. "You did get me the Asian chicken salad didn't you? There's always enough of that for two people. Anyway, I'm way too nervous about my date with Phillip tonight to eat much of anything."

"That's right. Tonight's the big night." Jane was happy to see Annie so excited.

"I brought three different outfits for you guys to vote on, okay? I just have no idea of what to wear. I'm not totally sure where he's taking me, but I bet it's going to be pretty nice. I don't want to be too casual, but I sure don't want to overdress either. That would be worse."

"We'll take care of you, boss. Don't worry," Grace said.

Jane glanced down the hallway and set the bag on the counter. "How are you doing, Grace? How's your nose?" Jane peered at Grace's face. The bruising below her eyes was still pretty bad. She kind of looked like a raccoon, but there wasn't much swelling, and her nose looked like it was in its original position.

"It isn't too bad. At first, I was worried I'd look like a prize fighter in my wedding pictures, but the doctor assured me he could set it back just fine." She shivered and grimaced. "Let me tell you, that is something I never want to do again. It was worse than the actual wreck."

"I'm glad you're back."

"Me too," Annie called out as she shut the display cooler door.

Jane winked at Grace. "If you were ever thinking about asking for a raise, now would be the time to do it. You have no idea how much Annie missed you."

"Don't give her any big ideas," Annie laughed.

"Hello all!" Rodney came out of the salon room. He was wearing a color cape and had little pieces of foil layered over his head.

"I didn't know you were going to do highlights. You should've waited till I got here to help." Jane picked the lunch bag back up and walked toward the work room. She hoped he hadn't noticed that she was avoiding looking him in his eyes. "Um, do you have time to eat before you need to rinse?"

"Let's see." Rodney tapped his chin with his finger. "I think I have just enough time for you to tell my why you took it upon yourself to fire every single person at the construction site this morning. That's exactly how much time I have."

Jane's mouth fell open. "How in the world do you know about that?"

"It is kind of like magic or witchcraft or something, the way that boy knows what's going on," Annie said.

"What happened?" Grace leaned against the counter.

Jane's eyes filled with tears. "It was terrible. I didn't mean to stop the work, but that awful Mark was just so rude this morning. He was yelling all these racial slurs at his workers and they were just taking it. I mean, one guy made a mistake with the tile and Mark was all over him." Jane knew she was babbling, but could not stop herself. "And it was obvious that everyone was scared of him, I mean, they would all flinch whenever he laughed or yelled. What was I supposed to do? Just stand there and be okay with him doing all of that on my property, my home?"

"Hush, hush." Rodney put his arm around her shoulders. "No way should you stand there and let that man abuse his workers. You did the right thing. It's okay." Jane looked up at him, the foil in his hair reflecting the light. "You aren't mad?"

Rodney laughed. "Actually, I'm delighted! It's usually me that causes chaos and delay, and I must say that I really am enjoying it being you this time. Who knows? I could get used to being the calm, rational one."

"How did you know?"

"Jeff called me after Mark called him. I told him that I did not even need to know the details and that I agreed with your decision one hundred percent. If you say that we have to have a new supervisor, then we have to have a new supervisor. No questions asked."

"What did he say?" Jane shifted the lunch bag to one hand and wiped her eyes with the other.

"Oh, he went on and on about how hard it was going to be to find someone, blah, blah, blah. The long shot is that he will have some guys go back out to secure the site and materials today. He'll call us as soon as he can find a replacement."

"See?" Annie patted Jane on the back. "You were worried for nothing."

"I think you're a hero," Grace said. "If everybody stood up when they saw that kind of behavior, we would have a lot less of it."

Jane took a deep breath. "I sure don't feel like a hero. The workers wouldn't even face me, and they just left with him."

"Probably to another work site, don't you think?" Rodney stepped out of the way and motioned for Jane to pass him in the narrow hall. "What other choice do they have? He's the one that gets them work."

"It's a shame, but Rodney's right." Annie followed Jane to the work room. "I know you were told all these workers were legal, but I am willing to bet that some have slipped through the crack. They would be almost completely dependent on men like Mark."

Jane passed out the take-out containers while Grace grabbed some Diet Cokes from the refrigerator. "I should probably have kept my big mouth shut."

"No. You did the right thing, Jane," Grace said.

"It isn't like the delay is going to cost you that much more time." Annie scooped half of the large salad onto a paper plate and handed it to Grace. "You still haven't even come up with a name."

"Not yet?" Grace laughed.

"Oh, Rodney has come up with a ton of names, but I refuse to work at a place called 'Rodney's Hair-o-Rama.' I mean, I couldn't live with myself." Jane pretended not to notice Rodney frowning at her.

"I have the perfect idea!" Grace clapped her hands together. "Why not make up a suggestion box and let your clients give you name ideas? You're bound to come up with something you can use."

"That isn't a bad idea," Annie said. "You could even give out a gift certificate for the winner."

"We could set out the box for one week and see what we get. Maybe by then, the contractor issue will be sorted out, and we can get back on track. We do need a name pretty soon or we're never going to have the front door sign done on time," Jane agreed.

"See?" Rodney said. "You didn't wreck anything at all." He paused dramatically. "Now that's over, do you want to know the real news of the day?"

"What?" Jane and Annie asked in unison, Grace had her mouth full.

"I ordered it." Rodney grinned. "I put it on overnight delivery and it will be here tomorrow."

"What?" Grace asked, swallowing.

"I finally ordered the one pair of scissors that I have lusted after since school. I decided it was high time that I did something nice for myself and I bought them this morning." Rodney's eyes lit up as he smiled. "Take a look at this." He pulled a brochure from his back pocket. It had been well read; the paper was so thin along the folds that it was starting to come apart.

Annie reached out and took it from him. "Why Rodney, I haven't seen you this excited about anything in ages." She held the front of the brochure up so Grace could see the color photograph of the scissors.

"It's the Razor's Edge 300 series with Dragon Platinum design." Rodney grinned.

Grace and Annie were trying to look suitably impressed but were failing. Jane decided some explanation was in order. "Think about a master chef and his knife. Think about a surgeon and his scalpel. Now mix in a little King Arthur's Excalibur, and you'll begin to see what the Razor's Edge 300 means to Rodney."

"Very nice." Annie smiled and handed the brochure back to Rodney. "It's good to splurge on yourself sometimes."

"It was a bit of a splurge, but I finally decided that I am worth twelve-hundred-dollar scissors."

Jane choked on her Diet Coke. She knew the scissors weren't cheap but she never imagined they were that much. She sure knew how much business Rodney usually did in a week. Splurge was not the word. "Those scissors cost twelve hundred dollars? What is John going to say about your little shopping spree?"

"I don't know and I don't care." Rodney slid the brochure back into his pocket. "He is apparently just fine with going off and doing his thing. It's about time that I went off and did mine."

Jane thought about arguing with him but decided it would do no good. Besides, part of her agreed that John had a couple of things coming to him. He might be getting off cheap if all Rodney charged on their joint account was twelve hundred dollars.

Annie's cell phone rang. She looked at the caller ID display and whispered. "It's Phillip!"

"Answer it!" Grace said.

Annie flipped open the phone as she walked out of the room. Rodney got up to follow her, but Jane pulled him back onto the stool. "Give her some privacy."

After a couple of minutes, Annie came back into the room with her cell phone pressed against her ear. "Did you find her car?"

Rodney raised his eyebrows. Jane shrugged in confusion.

"And are you sure that she left last night? Oh, I see." Annie walked to the counter, turned and walked back toward the doorway.

Jane knew the situation was serious whenever Annie started pacing the small work room. Any anxiety Annie felt was usually walked out between the buckets of cut flowers. Rodney swore that in the right light you could actually see a faint path worn into the ancient linoleum.

"No, no. Please, let me know if there is anything, anything at all we can do for you. Phillip, I am so sorry." Annie closed the cell phone slowly.

"Well? What is going on?" Grace demanded.

Annie's eyes were wide as she looked at Rodney. "Phillip called to say that he had to cancel our date because Bethany is missing."

"Missing?" Rodney stood up. "What do you mean?"

"What did he say?" Jane placed her hand on Rodney's arm.

"He said that Bethany was not at work this morning. Her car was in still in the parking lot."

"Wait a second," Grace said. "Is this the Bethany that's Rodney's client? The cute little blonde one?"

Annie nodded. "Apparently, Bethany and Phillip worked late last night. He said he left her at the office and went home after eleven. When he came back this morning, her car was still parked in her usual space, but she wasn't anywhere to be

A Discriminating Death

found." Annie took a deep breath. "Phillip said that her purse and cell phone were on her desk."

Jane closed her eyes. "She called the house yesterday afternoon."

"What?" Rodney turned to her. "What did she say?"

"I didn't answer," Jane groaned. "You and John were being so sulky and nasty that I was hiding out in my room. I heard the phone ring but there was no way I was going to venture out to the kitchen and risk meeting either of you. I figured you guys would get it or it could go to voicemail."

"I heard it too," Rodney said. "I didn't want to run into John so I didn't answer it either. I never even gave it another thought." He turned to Jane. "Did you check the message?"

"I checked it this morning. All Bethany said was that she was going to mail Phillip's family information to you so you could get started on the project. She said she tried to call your cell, but your phone was off."

"Did you save the message? What if that was the last call she made?" Grace's eyes were wide, magnifying the dark circles underneath. "You need to tell Phillip and the police. They can at least use it as a time line."

Rodney sat down. "Surely, there's more to go on. I mean, the Restin office has to have security of some kind. Someone must have seen something."

Annie had not stopped pacing. "Phillip said that you have to swipe a badge to enter the building but not to leave it. Security checked the logs for last night and it has both him and Bethany swiping in about five minutes apart and that's it. No one else was there and there's no way to tell when she left."

"He's already called the police, right?" Jane asked.

"Yes, but they say they can't start an investigation until she has been gone for forty-eight hours. The detective told Phillip that they would start checking things out sooner though, unofficially of course."

"Call John. See what he knows." Grace nodded at Rodney.

Rodney snarled in disgust. "Please. John won't know anything and even if he did, I would be the last person he'd tell."

"One car wreck and a couple of days off work, and I am totally out of the loop."

"I'll fill you in later." Jane frowned at Grace. "Right now, let's hear more about Bethany."

"There really isn't much more," Annie said. "I asked Phillip if there was anything we could do, and he said he'd call me when he had any news. He sounded devastated. His voice was breaking."

"I can't believe this," Rodney said. "I just can't believe that no one knows where she is."

"Someone has to know where she is." Jane meant to be reassuring, but knew her words sounded ominous. If anything serious had happened to Bethany, then it was possible that only one person would ever know where she was. Rodney glanced at her, and she knew he was thinking the same thing.

"His office is near downtown, right?" Grace said.

"Right." Annie stopped pacing and looked at her assistant.

"Maybe some other office building has video surveillance and got some shots of Bethany leaving. It could be a good lead."

"All the more reason to get the police involved as soon as possible. They'll check out every lead they get." Annie flipped open her cell phone. "I'd better go ahead and call Phillip and let him know about the timing of the message at Rodney's. It's not much, but it's all we have to offer for now."

Jane knew that if Phillip and the police had Bethany's cell phone, they already knew the timing of the call. Jane also knew that Annie felt the need to offer some kind of help to Phillip. Her desire to talk to him again was written all over her face.

The timer rang from the next room. Rodney reached up and pulled a foil wrapper out of his hair. "Jane, will you please get this stuff off of my head? I want to go home."

A Discriminating Death

Jane shampooed Rodney's hair slowly, massaging his scalp and trying to get him to relax. It didn't work. His muscles were tense and his eyes tightly closed while she rubbed a mango flavored deep conditioner into his hair. She finally rinsed him and watched as he rubbed a towel over his head.

"Are you ready to go?" He ran a comb through his hair and quickly wiped down his station.

"I'm ready." Jane nodded once. "Let me drive. We can leave your car here for one night." First, she wanted to get Rodney home, then, she wanted to fix a cold glass of ice water, find a dark spot to sit, and call Brian. He deserved to know about Bethany's disappearance, and she was desperate to hear his voice.

Chapter Seven

"And that's when the trouble started. Yes, it was real murder and blood-shed trouble, not one of your little puny feud fights. On black nights in the dark of the moon the Melungeons come a-raiding the farm people – man, woman and child – and slipping back to the ridges. They left burning barns and houses behind them, they killed the stock and fired the crops in the fields.
   Mighty few whites lived to tell of it when them devils had been around."[viii]

   Jane had nightmares about Bethany and would bet that Rodney did too. It didn't help that John was under foot again this morning.
   John's work schedule was really wearing Jane out. She sure wished the criminal element in the Save Our Nature group kept a more consistent routine. She'd give anything to have John out watching the spiky-haired woman get up to mischief instead of having him here, carefully trying to avoid Rodney during breakfast. She didn't know how much longer she could take their efforts to step out of each other's way while they poured coffee and made toast. Jane had to wait till

they finally sat at the table ignoring one another before she felt it was safe to navigate the kitchen and fix her cereal. Why one of them didn't break down and start eating out more often was beyond her. Maybe neither wanted to give up their home territory.

Jane looked at John, face hidden behind the newspaper to her right, and then at Rodney, staring into his cup of coffee on her left. Rodney had not asked John one question about Bethany's disappearance.

Jane had caught John in the living room while Rodney was taking a shower and had questioned him herself. He admitted that he'd heard the news but insisted he was not involved in the search effort. He told her not to worry and that the police were already taking it seriously even thought the official time period to start an investigation had not yet passed. Jane was not much comforted by his news or by the fact that he didn't ask how Rodney was holding up during all of this.

The only sounds in the kitchen were John's rustling newspaper and Rodney's chewing. Jane felt Zeke rub against her legs as she finished her cereal in silence. The single bright spot to the day was that it was finally the third Tuesday of the month. Brian would be coming in for his regular appointment at eleven. She'd give him a trim and then they would go out for lunch. She thought about his face when she shampooed his hair. His eyes would close and she could see him completely relaxed while she massaged his scalp.

"Are you ready?" Rodney stood up suddenly, startling Jane out of her daydream. "We need to get going. I have a nine o'clock."

"I'm almost ready. I just need to feed Zeke and then I can hit the road."

Rodney rinsed his plate and mug and placed them in the dishwasher. John never stirred from behind his newspaper screen. Rodney reached for Jane's cereal bowl and washed it for her while she shook dry cat food in Zeke's dish. Zeke emerged from under her chair and sniffed distastefully at his bowl before slowly settling himself under the kitchen table. He turned his head and pointedly ignored Jane as she reached down to pet him. Jane thought he protested too much, she knew his bowl would be licked clean by the time she got home tonight.

Jane opened the garage door and stepped into the humid morning. "How did you sleep last night?"

"Not well," Rodney admitted. "I had a couple of nightmares."

"Do you want to talk about them?"

"There's not much to talk about, just more of the same."

Jane unlocked her car doors, and they climbed in. She carefully backed out of the driveway and headed toward Bloom's.

Rodney turned the air conditioning on full blast and pointed the vent blowers at his face. "I know you must have asked John about Bethany. What did he say?"

"I did ask him." Jane turned one of the middle blowers back towards her. "He didn't really have anything to say at all."

Rodney snorted. "Oh, you mean he didn't have anything to say to that he wanted repeated to me. Nice."

"No, I really don't think he knows any of the details." Jane was frustrated that she was defending John. She was really irritated with him. If only he would open his mouth and talk to Rodney, things would be a lot better, but no. It seemed that he was more interested in keeping his secrets and his job than in keeping his relationship.

"Forget about it," Rodney sighed. "I don't want to even think about John right now." He paused. "However, I can't stop thinking about Bethany. I can't imagine where she could be, but I'm positive she didn't go there willingly. Why else would she leave her car downtown and then miss work the next morning? The longer she's gone, the less chance they have of finding her, or her body."

Susan Dorsey

***

Grace held the door open for them as they walked up the front steps to Bloom's. "Well? Have you heard anything else about Bethany? Did you at least talk to John?"

Rodney brushed by her and headed toward the salon room. Jane watched him walk down the hall and then turned to meet Grace's earnest gaze. "We don't know anything new. Rodney didn't talk to John, but I did, and he didn't have any information for me."

Grace shut the door behind Jane. "I just can't get the image of Bethany out of my head. I didn't know her really well, but I did like her. Annie told me that Bethany was the one that got us the Restin account. It was really nice of her to go out of her way like that."

Jane noticed that Grace was talking about Bethany in the past tense. She cringed but didn't correct her.

Annie walked in, tying her green apron around her waist. "Do you have any news about Bethany? Did Rodney and John ever talk?"

"No and no. No news and no conversation between those two." Jane walked over to the consultation table and sat down in one of the upholstered chairs. "I wish there was something we could do."

Annie sat down beside her. "I'm going to call Phillip today and check on him. Maybe he can tell me if there are any new developments."

"He'll know before anyone else," Grace said. "I wonder when they'll announce it on the news. You'd think that the police would want all eyes looking out for her, you know?"

"I'll keep the radio on in the salon room," Jane said. "You guys keep the television on in the work room. Maybe we'll find out something that way." She pressed her hands against her legs and stood up. "I have a feeling it is going to be a long day."

A Discriminating Death

"It's almost nine now," Annie said. "I think I'll wait till closer to ten to call Phillip. I hate to bother him first thing in the morning."

"I don't think a call from you would be bothering him," Grace urged. "He likes you, right? I bet a call from you is just what he needs about now."

"Maybe, but I am still waiting till ten, so you just have to wait too. Flattery is welcome but won't change anything. Besides, we have actual work to do around here if you're going to get out the door with the morning deliveries."

"Fine," Grace conceded. "Still, I'm not leaving on my route till you call Phillip."

The front door opened, and Rodney's first client walked in. Jane winced when she saw it was Andrea Clark. Jane knew Rodney was not fond of the older woman but tolerated her for the multiple referrals she sent his way. She was formal to the point of refusing to be on a first name basis with anyone she paid to do anything. She was extremely particular and often condescending with her instructions on just exactly how Rodney was supposed to do her hair. Jane had often wondered why she kept coming to Rodney, seeing how she felt she had to direct him every step of the way. She sure hoped the rest of Rodney's day was going to be better than his morning.

Jane stood up and smiled. She knew it was petty of her but she used first names whenever she could around Ms. Clark. "Good morning, Andrea. Rodney is just getting set up for you, come on back." She followed his client down the hallway. She had a nine-fifteen to get ready for herself.

Rodney smiled like butter wouldn't melt in his mouth and proceeded to work his charm and magic. Jane prepped her work station and tried to not listen to Ms. Clark speak to Rodney as though he were the lowest of the hired help.

"Now, you know that last time, my color was just not right. It was a little too yellow and not enough golden. Do not make that mistake again. I will not tolerate those vultures at bridge club mocking my hair."

"We did use the exact same formula last time that we use every six weeks."

"Well, then there must have been something wrong with the way you put it on. Just don't let it happen again."

Rodney took a deep breath and draped a color cloth around her shoulders. She peered at him in the mirror. "You don't look well. Are you doing drugs? Are you sick? Do you have the HIV?"

"What?" Rodney gasped in surprise. "What are you talking about?"

"Those bags under your eyes. You look sick. Now, I know how your kind is and if you have a disease, you had better tell me right now. No offense, but I don't want you using scissors near me if you're sick."

Jane froze.

"You know how my kind is, do you?" Rodney's voice was low.

"Well, yes." Ms. Clark patted the sides of her hair, apparently oblivious to the effect of her words. "Now, I didn't mean to offend you, but I do have a right to know the truth. I am your customer."

Wide eyed, Jane turned to face Rodney's station. Rodney slowly unsnapped the color cape from Ms. Clark's neck.

"You are mistaken, ma'am. You most certainly are not my client, and you would not know the truth if it bit you on your pearly white bottom. Get out of my salon and never come back, you ignorant cow."

Jane's mouth fell open. She had never seen Rodney act like this. He had never once insulted a client. She was horrified but proud at the same time. She realized she was smiling as Ms. Clark's face turned red and she climbed awkwardly out of the styling chair.

"What do you think you are doing?" She sputtered in rage as she grabbed her purse. "Who do you think you are?" She didn't leave Rodney time to answer that question. "Who do you think I am? I am going to tell all my girlfriends about you. You will be ruined, do you hear me? Ruined!"

Amazingly, Rodney kept his mouth shut as he walked to the front door. Ms. Clark stormed after him. Jane ran after her.

Rodney opened the front door, bells jingling loudly and smiled at Ms. Clark once again. Annie and Grace had run to the front room to see what was going on. "Good-bye now, and remember, don't come back."

Ms. Clark spun toward Annie and pointed a manicured finger at her. "And you! You let this kind of people work here and treat your customers like this? I'm telling everyone about you too. You'll regret letting him abuse me."

"Get out." Annie's voice was flat. "Get out now."

Ms. Clark glared once more at Rodney and then stomped out of the shop. Rodney and Jane watched while she slammed her Mercedes door closed and peeled out of the parking lot.

"What was that about?" Annie asked. "Tell me why I just kicked a woman out of my shop."

"She deserved it, Annie," Jane said. She knew she shouldn't be smiling, but she just couldn't help it. "Good job for you sticking up for Rodney even though you didn't know what was going on."

"Yeah, thanks Annie." Rodney grinned as he placed one hand on his heart and draped the other over his forehead. "Good heavens, I think I'm going to faint! I have never kicked a customer out before!"

"What happened?" Grace was almost hopping from foot to foot with excitement.

"I guess it was just the final straw, so to speak," Rodney said.

"That old biddy saw Rodney was not looking fresh as a daisy." Jane glanced at her friend. "And who would after everything he's been through this week? But instead of asking him what was wrong, she accused him of having HIV or doing drugs."

The smile slipped from Rodney's face. "She told me that she knew about 'my kind' and she didn't want me using scissors on her if I was sick."

"Oh dear Lord," Annie said. "I'm sure glad you kicked her out."

"She had no right to speak to you that way," Grace said.

"Good for you, Rodney. I am really proud of you!" Jane meant it.

"I'm just glad that I hadn't already started her color." Rodney laughed. "If I'd kicked her out of here with chemicals all over her head, she would have sued me for sure!"

The front door bell jingled again. Jane turned quickly hoping Ms. Clark wasn't back for more insults. Fortunately, it was her nine-fifteen, right on time.

"Hey, Jennifer, come on in," Jane sighed in relief.

"What's going on?" Jennifer looked at their stunned faces.

"Rodney just kicked out his first client!" Jane laughed.

"We are all so proud of him!" Annie said.

Jennifer patted Rodney on the shoulder. She'd been coming to Jane for two years and was very fond of Rodney. "Tell me all about it while Jane makes me beautiful. That must have been some doozey of a client for you to lose your cool."

"Girl, you have no idea," Rodney said as he sauntered to the salon room.

* * *

Jane finished cutting Jennifer's hair just as Rodney finished telling her not only about his exploits, but also about how Jane had fired the construction supervisor at the salon site.

"Watch out for us, honey. Apparently, Jane and I no longer take crap from anyone." Rodney spun in fast circles in his cutting chair.

"I should say not!" Jennifer laughed. "But you guys might want to rein it in a little bit. How on earth are you going to have your grand opening without an actual salon to open?"

Rodney waved his hand in the air dismissively while Jane shook the cut hair from Jennifer's cape. "Oh, we'll have a new site supervisor by next week."

"Yeah, that's not our biggest problem right now." Jane thought about Bethany and John, and then added, "Well, not our biggest work problem anyway. We still don't have a name for the salon."

"You two are getting down to the wire," Jennifer said. "Soon you'll be reduced to just drawing one out of a hat."

Rodney put his foot on the floor to stop the spinning chair. "You're right Jennifer. Grace told us we ought to make a suggestion box and give away a gift certificate for the winning name." He glanced up at the clock between the work stations. "I've got another thirty minutes before my next one. I can get started now."

"Please Jennifer, if you have any suggestions that do not include the words 'Rodney, palace, or o'rama,' we would sure owe you one." Jane picked up her hair dryer as Rodney started rooting through the bottom cabinet of his work station.

By the time Jane had finished drying and curling Jennifer's hair, Rodney had covered an empty glove box with tissue paper from Annie's work room. He moved the magazines from a small table beside the dryer chair and gently placed the box on top. Jane watched as he propped up a sign reading, 'Name The Salon Contest' written in his beautiful calligraphy. He finished by fanning out several small squares of paper and placing two pens on the table top.

"Not bad." Jennifer was looking at the back of her head with a small hand held mirror, angling it right and left to see Jane's work.

"I know! That box only took me ten minutes to make." Rodney smiled. "Come on, be our first contributor. You could win a twenty-five dollar gift certificate to, well, whatever we call ourselves come October!"

"I'm kicking in a twenty-five dollar gift certificate to Bloom's too." Annie appeared in the doorway wiping her hands on her apron. "I can't take any more bickering about it. I don't really care what they name the salon, I just want it over with."

Jane accepted a check from Jennifer and unsnapped the cutting cape. "Just remember, nothing with the word 'Rodney' in it."

"I can hear you!" Rodney sang out as he handed Jennifer a pen.

"Okay, okay. You guys really know how to put a girl on the spot." She looked thoughtfully at Rodney and then Jane. "Do I have to put my name on the suggestion?"

"Yes! How else would we know who to give the grand prize to?" Jane laughed. "Come on, your ideas can't be any worse than," she looked at Rodney, "um, the ones we have heard so far."

"Okay. No peeking, though, 'til the contest is over." Jennifer turned her back to the room. She pressed the square of paper up against the wall and wrote quickly before folding it in half. She dropped it into the opening at the top of the box. "All right, suggestion number one is in."

"Thanks Jennifer." Jane smiled. "Do you want to go ahead and make your next appointment, or do you want to give me a call later?"

"Put me down for nine-fifteen again, in let's say, two months? When will that be?"

Jane grabbed the pink- and white-columned appointment book and flipped through the pages. "You are pushing it. That's the middle of October. With any luck we'll see you at our new place. I'll make sure and send out reminder postcards with our new address."

"And our new name." Rodney smiled.

A Discriminating Death

Grace leaned into the room. "Annie. It's ten o'clock on the dot. Don't you have a phone call to make?"

Annie tightened her lips and nodded to Grace. "Okay, now is as good as ever."

Jane walked Jennifer to the front door and then went back to clean her station. Rodney was in the dryer chair. His legs were crossed and he was swinging his foot so hard that the chair was rocking.

"Do you think Phillip has heard anything?"

"If he has, we'll find out soon enough." Jane pulled the broom out from the side of her station and started to sweep. She always liked this part of the job, the tidying up after one happy client and the getting ready for the next. She liked putting things in order. It was relaxing for her to take a quick break and just focus on the motion of the broom.

"There's been nothing on the radio news." Rodney interrupted her thoughts. "Surely if the police had found her body they would have reported something."

Jane stopped sweeping. "Rodney, we don't know that things have gone as badly as that. We don't know they're looking for her body. Let's try to keep thinking positively about this. Bethany is a resourceful woman. Just try to imagine the best-case scenario, okay?"

Rodney stopped swinging his foot. "Jane, you and I know that sometimes the best-case scenario *is* finding the body."

Jane leaned on the broom and frowned. Rodney was right, but she wasn't going to admit it to him. Not in the state of mind that he was in. John had never shared too many of his work stories with them, especially not in any detail, but he hadn't had to. The news was bad enough. Knoxville, like any bustling city, had seen its share of unthinkable crimes. Jane actually tried not to watch the news at all any more, preferring to get her weather forecast on the internet.

Annie walked quietly into the room. Grace followed on her heels.

"Did you get to talk to him? What did he say?" Rodney rose to his feet.

"I did get to talk to him, but there wasn't much more to tell." Annie paused. "He said the police were going to have a news conference this afternoon around three. You know, show her picture and provide a hot line for tips. He and Cindy were going to be there offering a one hundred thousand dollar reward for any information."

"Do they have any new information? Anything at all?" Grace asked.

"Phillip hasn't heard anything," Annie sighed. "He is just a complete wreck. His voice is hoarse and he talks either too fast or he takes strange breaks between his sentences. He must not have slept at all last night. I wish I could be with him through all of this. Cindy didn't sound like she was helping things at all. I could hear her in the background yelling at some poor secretary about her coffee being cold."

"Is there anything we can do?" Jane asked, knowing that there wasn't.

"Phillip did say that the police will want to talk to anyone that saw Bethany over the weekend." Annie looked at her friend. "You and Rodney should call the station and tell them about the message and her state of mind on Saturday night."

"Her state of mind was fine," Rodney groaned. "*She* was fine."

"Still, you never know what helps," Grace said. "You should call."

The bells at the front door rang. Rodney rubbed his eyes and took a deep breath.

"Thanks for letting us know, Annie. We'll keep the radio on and listen for the police conference."

"Yoo hoo! Anyone home?" Rodney's client called down the hallway. Fortunately, it was one he actually liked this time.

"We're back here running our mouths," Rodney called out. "Come join us."

A Discriminating Death

His client, Emma, walked in and placed her purse on his work station. "What's going on?"

"Nothing good. Sit down and I'll tell you all about it, but first Jane and I have a phone call to make."

"No more talking for us, Grace. We've got to get you out on deliveries." Annie gently pushed Grace out the door.

"Do you want to do the honors?" Rodney held the phone out for Jane.

Jane took it from his hands. She thought it was pointless to bother the police with what little information they had, but still, at least they would be doing something to help find Bethany. She dialed the station number from memory. John's precinct would be as good as any. The call was answered on the first ring. Jane turned to face the window and explained that she wanted to make a statement concerning Bethany Collins.

Rodney and Emma listened as Jane recounted the events of the weekend, when they had parted with Bethany on Saturday, and the time of the phone message on Sunday afternoon. Jane then handed the phone to Rodney so he could confirm the details.

"That is just awful that you two knew her," Emma whispered as Rodney spelled his name for the detective. Jane wished that people wouldn't keep talking about Bethany in the past tense. It was if their subconscious already knew the truth.

Rodney finished his statement and assured the detective they would be available for further information if he needed it. He hung up the phone and frowned. "I'm glad that's over with. Thanks for waiting, Emma."

"No problem, sweetie."

Jane finished cleaning and looked up at the clock. She tried to push thoughts of Bethany aside. At this point, she had done everything in her power to help. If there was an organized hunt for her, Jane and Rodney would be on the frontlines, but until then, there was nothing else Jane could think of.

Her next client would be Brian. She was thankful she had something positive to look forward to, especially after the past two days. She glanced up at Rodney at the shampoo sink. There was no way she could leave him on his own for lunch today. Once again she was going to lose out on the opportunity for a quiet moment with Brian, but she couldn't go without inviting her best friend. Still, she did get to run her fingers through Brian's hair in about ten minutes. That was better than nothing.

* * *

Brian was right on time as always. He greeted Jane with a smile and a kiss to the cheek. This was a first. He'd kissed her before, but never as part of a 'hello' and never in public. Jane felt herself blush as she settled him into the shampoo chair and gently reclined him into the sink.

She watched his face relax as she scrubbed his hair and massaged his scalp. She made sure to use an extra round of conditioner, even though he certainly did not need it. It gave her an excuse to touch him a little while longer. Jane caught Rodney's eye as she dried Brian's hair with a fresh towel, he gave her a small smile as he walked Emma out of the room.

Jane settled Brian in her stylist chair. She glanced at the door to make sure Rodney was still gone then she leaned close to Brian's ear. She inhaled his cologne and forced herself to concentrate. "Brian, is it okay if we ask Rodney to come to lunch with us today? I really hate to impose, but I just don't want to leave him alone right now."

Brian turned to her so that their faces were almost touching. Jane felt her heart beat against her chest. Instead of kissing her, Brian just smiled. "That's okay. We can be alone another time."

He turned back to the mirror as Jane got her scissors out. She was carefully trimming his neckline when Rodney returned.

"Do you mind if I turn this off?" Rodney asked as he switched off the radio. "I just can't take any more soft rock this morning. Now that we know there's not going to be a press conference till three, I'd just rather not listen to anything if it's all the same to you."

"What's the conference going to be about?" Brian spoke without moving. Jane had once inadvertently cut his ear during a trim. It was a complete accident brought on by nerves and Jane had apologized repeatedly. Apparently Brian had forgiven it but not quite forgotten it.

"Bethany. The police are going to make her a formal missing person and show her photograph. Annie called Phillip this morning and he told her the news."

"I sure hate this." Brian looked at Jane's reflection. She knew he was thinking the worst too. Jane doubted he had seen many happy endings in his line of business.

Jane brushed the stray hair off his neck and unclipped the cape. Brian's regular visits meant that there was very little to trim each time, which was nice because it also meant they had more time for lunch.

"Hey Rodney." Jane tried to make her voice sound casual. "Why don't you come to lunch with us? You're next one isn't till one-thirty."

Brian stood up and brushed off his black pants. As usual he was impeccably dressed for his work. Jane couldn't imagine him in blue jeans and a sweatshirt. "Yeah Rodney, come join us. We're going to try out this new Thai place that opened up in Turkey Creek."

Jane put her hand to her ear. "Listen Rodney, I think I hear a veggie spring roll calling your name!"

"Thanks, but no. I appreciate it, but I think I'll stay here and keep Annie company. I need to reorganize the supply closet anyway. I think we are running low on auburn color R5. And of course, I don't want to miss my special delivery."

"And what would that be?" Brian asked.

"Rodney has ordered a very special pair of cutting shears," Jane said. "Very special." She turned to Rodney. "Are you sure you won't come?"

"Positive, positive. You kids run along and have fun." Rodney sat down in his stylist chair and peered into his mirror.

"Can we at least bring you anything back?" Brian asked.

"No thanks, we've got some frozen dinners in the store room. I'll just microwave one of those." Rodney ran his fingers through his hair and frowned a little at his reflection.

"Let me check with Annie and see if she wants anything." Jane glanced at Brian. "I'll meet you in the car."

"Aren't you forgetting something?" Rodney asked as he turned toward the doorway. "Brian can't leave until he fills out a suggestion slip." He pointed dramatically to the box. "Just tell us your idea for naming the salon and you can be on your way."

"What's this?" Brian asked.

"Let's just say we are getting desperate for some ideas," Jane said. "If we pick yours, then you win a couple of gift certificates."

"Okay, just give me a minute to think." Brian picked up a pen as Jane left to find Annie. She heard her talking on the phone at the front desk.

"I'd be glad to take care of that for you." Annie held the phone in the crook of her neck as she wrote on a small order pad. "Add a dozen pink balloons. I think that'll be great. All right, thank you."

She hung up the phone and looked at Jane. "Baby shower this Friday."

"Thai food this afternoon," Jane said. "Do you want us to bring you something back?"

"No thanks. I've got a Healthy Choice in the freezer, I'll just grab that." Annie looked toward the hallway. "Is Rodney going with you?"

"I invited him, but he refused. I thought he needed to get out, you know, get a change of scenery for a while."

"I'll keep an eye on him while you're gone." Annie squeezed Jane's arm. "You just keep your eye on Brian."

Jane was excited to get to talk with Brian alone, but she felt a twinge of guilt about leaving her friends. Not only was Rodney heart-broken over John and now Bethany, but Jane knew that Annie was worried about Phillip. It had been so long since Annie had been interested in anyone. It hardly seemed fair that their relationship might be off before it ever got a chance to be on. Jane just wanted her friends to be as happy as she was, partly so she would not feel so guilty about being happy herself.

* * *

Brian's black car was as hot as an oven as Jane climbed into it. She had worn a short skirt and black hose because she had known she would see him. She had to keep shifting her weight to keep the hot leather of the seat from burning the backs of her thighs.

Brian reached out and held her hand as they sat at a red light waiting to turn left onto Turkey Creek Road. "How's Rodney holding up? What does John think about Bethany?"

"Who knows?" Jane felt herself start to tear up and turned to look out the passenger window. She didn't want to cry in front of Brian. "John and Rodney are in the middle of the worst fight they've ever had. They are either screaming at each other or giving each other the silent treatment. It has been going on for days now." She patted gently under her eyes with the tip of her ring finger; the last thing she wanted was for her mascara to run.

"How long have they been together?"

"It seems like forever, but really it's only been maybe five or six years."

"That's a long time. They have a lot vested in one another. I'm sure they'll find a way to work it out." Brian pulled the car into a parking spot across from the restaurant.

"I don't know." Jane shook her head, she hated that she couldn't tell Brian the truth about John's undercover assignment. It felt wrong to keep secrets from him, but she didn't really have a choice. "Rodney's pretty upset about John returning to work after recovering from getting shot last spring. He keeps having nightmares that he's attending John's funeral."

"I guess I can understand that. I don't think I could be married to a police officer. I can't imagine how they can just walk up to a random car they pulled over for speeding and ask to see someone's driver's license. Every stop they make could be their last."

"Thankfully, John isn't on patrol any more," Jane said. "He was when they were first starting to date. Rodney was relieved when John made detective. Oh, he'd joke around and call John a desk jockey, but still, we all know there's no such thing as a safe job in the police department. Now that John is back to work, it may just be too much for Rodney."

"They're going to have to decide what they want, Jane. There isn't much you can do to help them except keep listening to them. Thankfully, you are really good at that. They are lucky to have you. Come to think of it, I'm lucky too." Brian smiled, then leaned over and kissed her.

Jane closed her eyes and tried to put her arms around his neck. Unfortunately, she hadn't taken her seatbelt off and she was held firmly back in her seat.

He kissed her gently again and then laughed. "We'd better get out of here and inside the restaurant. Trust me when I say that people do not want to see their funeral director making out in the parking lot of Thai Delights."

A Discriminating Death

* * *

Jane floated through lunch. She waited to see what Brian ordered and then ordered the same thing so that when he kissed her good-bye it wouldn't be an awkward kiss, filled with competing spices.

They didn't talk about Bethany or John again. Instead, Jane told Brian about how she had fired their contractor and how Rodney had kicked out his client for being so homophobic.

Brian told her about a double funeral he'd performed years ago. The deceased couple was a young African American man who had married a young white woman. They'd had a two-year-old daughter that both sides of the family doted on during the service planning. But when the day of the funeral came, everyone showed their true colors. The grandparents from both sides started screaming racial slurs and trying to grab that poor child, claiming she was theirs. It was horrifying to watch. The little girl had no idea what was happening and she just screamed and screamed. Brian and his brother had finally been able to break up the fight, but only by threatening to call the police. He knew that the real reason for the feud was grief, but race sure added fuel to the fire.

"Did you ever find out what happened to that poor little girl her after the service?"

"No, I never did." Brian finished his spiced iced tea. "I can't imagine that she's had an easy time of it - what kid would after losing both parents? But I hope that her family was able to settle down."

"Was that the worst service you ever had to do?"

"Not by a long shot. There have been a few funerals we actually did have to call the cops on. One was a couple of sixty-year-old daughters at the funeral of their ninety-year-old mother. They were both drunk as skunks and started fighting over their mother's jewelry. One sister actually reached into the casket to grab a pearl necklace that the deceased had requested to be buried in. The other sister launched herself at her sibling, and the casket came crashing to the floor."

"Oh, that's horrible." Jane tried not to laugh.

"It could have been much worse. Thankfully, the deceased did not actually come out of the casket, and we were able to get everything set up again without having to disturb the body, but we did call the cops. Both sisters went into the drunk tank to dry out, but not before the police officer returned the necklace and we continued with the burial."

"And here I thought I had an interesting job." Jane smiled as the waitress laid the bill on the table.

Brian picked it up and pulled his wallet out of his coat pocket. He laid down enough cash to cover the bill and leave a good tip before standing and pulling Jane's chair out for her. Jane was sure she could get used to this kind of gentlemanly behavior. He even held the door open for her as they stepped out into the muggy afternoon.

"Storm clouds are coming in." Brian covered his eyes and gazed at the sky. "I think we're really going to be in for it this time."

"Let's get on back to the salon. I don't want you to have to drive back to work in the rain." Jane hurried to the car.

Brian held the door open for her as she slid in. It was even hotter than before, hot enough to take her breath away.

Jane pointed two air conditioner vents directly at her face and then turned on the radio. "Do you mind? They might have some weather updates."

Instead of the weather report, they heard the breathless voice of a reporter screaming into a microphone, straining to be heard over the sound of sirens. "The explosions rocked the construction site about twenty minutes ago. The fires are still burning and we do not know if anyone was still at the site when the destruction started. Officers are in conference with the site supervisor to determine if any worker is unaccounted for."

Jane felt cold as fear flooded through her. Brian reached down and turned up the volume.

"Do not try to drive near the riverfront park area downtown. You will not be able to get through. The fires are still burning out of control, and the police have the whole area blocked off." The reporter coughed into the microphone, the sound piercing on the car's stereo. "The police haven't officially announced who is responsible for the vandalism, but I can just make out a large sun shape spray-painted on a bull dozer, and one of the workers told me the letters 'S O N' were sprayed on the front gate this morning."

"We have to go back now!" Jane couldn't hide the desperation in her voice. Brian glanced at her in confusion and then put the car in drive.

The first heavy rain drops started just as Brian pulled onto the interstate. The rain, coming down in sheets, was almost blinding. Jane watched Brian's hands tighten on the wheel as he pulled around a semi truck that was spraying water across their windshield. Jane leaned back in her seat, relieved that the sound of the rain drowned out any chance for conversation.

Lightning flashed across the sky as Brian pulled up to the front door of Bloom's. "I have an umbrella. Let me walk you in!" He had to shout over the sound of thunder and the rain beating on the car roof.

"I'll just make a run for it. You don't need to get wet too!" She was starting to open the door when she realized that Brian had leaned over to kiss her good-bye. She turned and quickly kissed him as she reached for the door handle.

Brian grabbed her arm. The rain started to pour into the car, soaking her skirt. "If you need to talk to me, you can."

Jane looked him in the eye, nodded once, then darted for the front porch. It was only about five feet away, but she was completely drenched when she turned to wave good-bye.

She saw him wave through the blurry windshield, and

then he was gone. Thunder rumbled, and she turned to face the front door, trying to think positive thoughts. Maybe the rain might put out the fire downtown. Maybe, just maybe, Rodney had not heard the news.

She opened the door slowly. The bells jingled softly. Rodney flew into the front room, his black work smock open, flapping around him as he ran. Annie hurried behind him.

"I suppose you heard the news?" Rodney glared. "It seems that John has been a busy boy."

"Now Rodney, you don't know John was involved in this." Jane shivered in the air conditioning and brushed her wet bangs from her forehead.

"Even if he was involved, he's only doing his job. You're going to have to let him do it." Annie glared at Rodney. "Come off your high horse and call him. He'll tell you how involved he was."

"He's not going to tell me a thing. Not one thing," Rodney spat. "He's been lying to me for weeks. Why on earth would he start telling me the truth now? There's no way that I'm going to give him the satisfaction of calling him and begging for information."

"Let's just stop and think about this." Jane frowned. She didn't think that it was likely John would tell Rodney anything about the fires either. "Nobody was hurt, right? Maybe this is good news. Maybe, this is just what John needed to nail this group, and now he can quit undercover work."

"And do what?" Rodney rubbed his face with his hands. "What is he going to do next? Go back on the duty roster investigating robberies and arresting druggies? That's not much better." He plopped down at the consultation table and looked out at the rain lashing against the front window.

Annie sat down beside Rodney. Jane was too wet to sit without soaking the fabric-covered chairs, so she just stood behind Rodney and put her hands on his shoulders. "Maybe you and John need to talk to somebody. I bet a lot of couples

A Discriminating Death

with a spouse in the police department go through these kinds of things."

Rodney reached up and patted her hands. "A lot of police officers are divorced Jane, and now I know why. If we hadn't followed him last Thursday, I'd never have known any of this. I'd never have known to be scared when I heard about the fire today. What else do I not know? I just can't live my life wondering if every tragedy that's reported has anything to do with John."

"Rodney." Annie leaned forward. "You're never going to get any of this resolved without at least talking to him." She put her hand on his leg. "You have to talk to him. Jane's idea was a good one. If you don't want to talk to John by yourself, get a third party to help you out. Talk to a counselor who could see both sides of things. Just at least try, okay?"

"Is your phone still off?" Jane asked.

Rodney nodded.

"You can't expect John to keep trying to reach you when you won't even turn your phone on. Please, give him a chance."

Rodney sighed and pulled his phone out of his pants pocket. He turned it on and stared as the screen displayed the company logo and then a picture of Rodney and John standing next to each other in their kitchen. Almost immediately, the phone vibrated in his hand. "I do have a few messages."

"We'll leave you alone to listen to them." Annie tilted her head toward the hallway. Jane nodded and followed her to the salon room. She grabbed a towel and started to dry her hair.

Annie sat in Rodney's chair and closed her eyes. "I hope they can work this out. Rodney was actually shaking with fear when the news broke. He was helping me with an arrangement and dropped a vase on the floor. Glass is everywhere."

"I'll help you clean up," Jane said. Her cell phone rang. She pulled it out of her pocket and glanced at the screen. "It's John."

"What?" Annie sat up. "Answer it."

"John? I thought you'd be talking to Rodney."

Jane held her breath and listened. Annie watched her with alarm.

"Okay. You're sure everything is okay? We'll be there as soon as we can." Jane saw Annie start to speak and she held up one finger toward her. "Your guess is as good as mine, but I'll warn him."

She shut the phone and looked at Annie. "That was John."

"Well, yes. I gathered that. What on earth did he say?" Annie looked up as Rodney entered the room.

"I checked all my messages, and not one was from John."

"Um, Rodney?" Jane motioned to the dryer chair. "Can you have a seat for a minute please?"

Rodney's eyes narrowed, but he sat.

"John just called me. He's okay. He's actually at home right now. You see, there was a break-in."

Rodney stood up as if he had been sitting on a hot stove. "A break in? At my house?"

"What next?" Annie groaned.

"What happened?" Rodney's voice was barely a whisper.

"It seems that your favorite neighbor Bill, well, he noticed the door beside the garage was open and he figured he ought to go check on things, make sure that no rain water was coming in. He said he peeked inside and the place was . . ." Jane's voice trailed off as she looked at Rodney. His face was expressionless. "He said the place was wrecked."

"Bill."

Jane knew Rodney was imagining Bill standing close to John, offering his support right this very minute.

Rodney's mouth tightened. "Let's go." He turned to Annie. "We'll take the appointment book and reschedule people for tomorrow. Do you mind cleaning up for us?"

"No, no. Go on. Let me know what you find out," Annie said.

A Discriminating Death

"I'll drive," Jane said. "You can make the phone calls."

"It has to be that SON group. It seems that John has brought his work home with him, just fabulous."

"We don't know that, Rodney," Jane said. "Let's just go see what we find out, okay? And, um, John did say that we need to control ourselves in front of the other officers there. You know, not mention his current work?" Jane held her breath as she watched his face.

"Oh, honey. I am in complete control of myself. You just wait and see."

Annie stepped back to let him pass. Jane gave her a worried look and then followed Rodney out into the rain.

* * *

Jane drove Rodney's car as fast as she safely could on the wet streets while he flipped through the appointment book and called their afternoon clients. He told each client about the break-in and promised he'd let them know everything during their next session.

She pulled up to the curb in front of the house. Police cars were blocking the driveway, their lights off. It looked as if John could be hosting a work luncheon instead of a crime scene.

Rodney grabbed a large umbrella from his back seat and opened the door. He walked around to the driver's side and sheltered Jane from the rain while she climbed out. Jane squeezed his upper arm and they walked down the sidewalk to the front porch.

"Excuse me, no one is allowed to enter." The uniformed police officer guarding the front door moved closer to the doorway as if Jane and Rodney might try to dart past him.

"Oh, excuse me." Rodney's eyes sparkled dangerously. "This is my home. Is Detective Bishop about? I really must insist on speaking with him. Right now."

Jane tightened her grip on Rodney's arm while a gust of wind blew the rain sideways under the umbrella.

"Rodney?" John opened the front door. He nodded at the officer. "It's okay, Rick. This is my partner, Rodney, and our friend, Jane. Jane's been staying with us and she needs to come in too. I need them to look around and see if anything of theirs has been taken."

The officer stepped out of the way as Rodney brushed by him into the foyer. Jane scooted quickly behind him and saw her first glimpse of the wreckage that was their living room. It looked like a wind storm had blown through the house. Books were pulled off of shelves and tossed in a large pile in the floor.

Rodney stood perfectly still in the middle of the foyer. Jane leaned around him and groaned out loud when she saw the kitchen. Flour covered the floor. Cans and bags were piled on the table as though someone had stood in front of the cabinets and just thrown things over their shoulder.

Jane's heart raced when she saw the overturned cat dishes. "John? Where's Zeke?"

"He's okay," John said. "I found him hiding under your bed. I tried to get him out but he won't budge."

"Okay." Jane felt her heart rate slow down a little bit. "That's probably the safest place for him now."

"Where's Bill?" Rodney asked quietly.

John sighed. "He gave his statement, and now he's back home. You know he was just being a good neighbor, Rodney. He didn't have to come over here just because the basement door was open."

A policewoman carrying a camera walked into the foyer. "You folks can go on back to the bedrooms now. I've finished with the photos."

"Thanks, Becky." John nodded. He waved Rodney and Jane to the back wing of the house. Jane tried to slow her breathing down as she walked to the guest room. After losing

A Discriminating Death

so much in the fire last spring, she couldn't bring herself to care too deeply about material possessions, but there were a few personal things that she would hate to loose.

She braced herself for the worst and looked into her room. Almost everything had been pulled out of her dresser drawers and was now strewn over her bedspread. Her favorite photograph, the one of her and Deborah dressed in matching Easter dresses and sitting on the front stoop of their house, was on the floor. The glass was broken as if someone had stepped on it, but the photo looked intact.

"Can we touch things?" Jane looked at John.

"Yes, it's okay. They've finished dusting for prints, though I doubt they found much. I'm guessing our visitor wore gloves."

"Sure doesn't sound like some kids looking for stuff to hock." Rodney bent down and picked up a black high heeled shoe from the floor. "More like some group member looking for information about a new recruit, don't you think?"

John pulled Rodney to his feet. "You stop it right there. You don't know anything about anything. Got it? Now, if you don't think you can keep your mouth shut, then you can leave."

Before she knew what she was doing, Jane stepped between the two men. "Stop it!" She glared at John. "Rodney has a valid point and you know it. You can't kick him out." She spun to face Rodney. "And you. You have to keep your mouth shut. Don't make things worse."

"Don't make things worse?" Rodney laughed. "Honey, it doesn't get much worse than this. I don't even care what things they took. What I wanted most in this house is already gone." He stepped around Jane and leaned close to John. "What I wanted is to know that you are safe, John. That was all. It's too late now. You must have given yourself away somehow and your new friends decided they had to check you out. What are you going to do now, John? What are you going to do now that you have brought this destruction home, to my house?"

"I am going to handle things," John growled at him. Jane stepped back and almost fell across an overturned chair.

"You've done a knock-up job so far, detective. Good work, really." Rodney skirted past him and headed toward the master bedroom. Jane watched as John closed his eyes and took several deep breaths.

"John?" Jane held the wall for balance as she stepped over the empty dresser drawers. "Do you think he's right? Are you in danger?"

John looked up. "I don't think so Jane." He glanced into the hallway and closed the door. "This isn't how SON usually does things. It just doesn't feel right. I've already talked to my supervisor and she's letting me stay on assignment for a while longer. We're too close to quit now."

"Are you serious?" Jane couldn't believe it. "What if you're wrong? What if it was SON looking for the truth about you? You were the one who said these people were dangerous."

"They are Jane, they are. I know there's more going on than just the fire downtown. They're up to something else, something big, and I refuse to be scared away because of a random break-in."

"I hope you're right."

John opened the door and looked into the empty hallway.

"But if you're not right, John, what then? Are Rodney and I safe here?"

"You're safe. We're going to have the house under twenty-four-hour surveillance for a while, just till things calm down. You're perfectly safe here."

Jane looked around at the wreckage of her room and then back at John. He couldn't meet her eyes.

Chapter Eight

"*After the breaking out of the war, some few enlisted in the army, but the greater number remained with their stills, to pillage and plunder among the helpless women and children. Their mountains became a terror to travelers; and not until within the last half decade has it been regarded as safe to cross Malungeon territory.*"[ix]

Jane's alarm went off at eight. She thought about pressing the snooze button but decided she might as well get up anyway. There was no chance she'd get any more sleep. She sat up in bed and tried to scoot Zeke off of her pillow. He opened one eye, glared at her, and then closed it again.

She was still exhausted from all of the cleaning they had done yesterday. John had gone back to the station while she and Rodney had wielded brooms and trash bags. They had worked for hours and finally returned the house to a semblance of order.

About halfway through the cleaning, they realized the intruder didn't actually take much of anything. A few items were gone from Jane's small jewelry box, but most of her earrings and necklaces were found under a pile of her shirts.

Rodney was missing some cuff links and watches, but that was all. They reported the missing items to the police, even though it was obvious to them that someone had been rooting through their things trying to find something rather than take something. Jane wondered if they had found what they were looking for.

The kitchen clean-up took the longest. They threw out every last bit of food in the house, including the cans in the pantry and the frozen food. Rodney refused to keep anything that might have been touched by the intruder. Fortunately, Annie brought pizza and beer over for dinner. She stayed to help them reorganize their closets. Rodney had also insisted on washing every piece of his clothing that might have been handled by the intruder, and they had run laundry all night.

Now the morning sun was filtering in through the blinds, and Jane knew it was time to get up. If John was here, she wanted to talk with him before Rodney was awake.

She hopped in the shower and then pulled on a pair of khaki pants and a crisp white shirt and some brown flats. She pulled her auburn hair into a short pony tail and rubbed on her foundation. She could touch up her make-up and hair later at work.

Jane carefully opened the guest room door and listened for the sounds of anyone stirring around in the kitchen. Zeke darted between her legs and headed off for breakfast. She closed the door behind him and walked down the hallway.

She could see the blankets folded beside the pillow on the sofa. John had obviously come home after she and Rodney were asleep, but there was no sign he was here now. Jane breathed a little easier as she peeked into the empty kitchen. She did want to talk to him, but she didn't think her nerves could handle another fight this morning. John must not have been up to it either; he had to know Rodney would be on the war path.

As if her thoughts had conjured him, Rodney came sauntering into the kitchen. He looked at the cold coffee pot and pursed his lips. "Jane, what do you say about grabbing a scone and a latte on the way in to the shop?"

Jane nodded. "Let me just feed Zeke, and we can go."

* * *

They finished their breakfast in the car and arrived at Bloom's a few minutes before their first appointments.

Annie greeted them at the front door. She smiled as she handed Rodney a small cardboard box. "This came yesterday after you went home. I meant to bring it to your house last night, but in all the excitement, I forgot."

"Come on, open it." Jane wanted to see what a pair of twelve-hundred-dollar shears looked like. She really wanted to hold them but figured that she shouldn't ask until Rodney had a chance to use them first.

"Okay, okay, don't rush me." Rodney walked toward the counter and placed the box beside the cash register. He pulled at the edge of the packing tape and peeled it off. The box top sprang open. Annie and Jane leaned around Rodney's shoulder to get a better look.

Rodney lifted a black velvet bag out of the box. Inside was a black leather holster cradling the scissors. Rodney wiped his hand on his pants and then slid the shears out into the light.

Jane had to admit the shears were a thing of beauty. The platinum coating gave the blades a bluish tint as they reflected the lamplight. The grip looked large enough to accommodate a man's fingers comfortably. There was even a curved thumb rest for greater control. The longer she looked at the scissors, the more jealous she grew. "Who's going to get the first cut?"

Rodney winked at her. "You look like you could use a trim."

Jane grinned. "We can do it this afternoon. We both have an opening at three."

Rodney carefully slipped the shears back into the holster and set them on the counter. He reached into the box and pulled out a large manual and a bottle of oil wrapped in a lint-free cleaning cloth.

"Do you really have to read that whole book to learn how to use them?" Annie asked. "What could you possibly need to know?"

"Lots of things, like cleaning, and storing, and daily maintenance." Rodney patted the top of the book. "These scissors are a work of art and require respect."

"Start reading. I want you ready to go by three," Jane said.

Grace came around the corner carrying a silk arrangement. "How are you guys doing this morning? Annie told me about the break-in. I just couldn't believe it. You two just don't have any luck."

"It could be worse," Rodney said as he closed the box lid and pressed the packing tape down. "Not much was taken."

The front door opened, and Rodney's first client, Liz, walked in. "Good morning, all. What's going on?"

"You won't believe it, but we'll tell you anyway." Rodney tucked the box under his arm and led the way to the salon room as Jane's client walked in. She waved her on back to the salon room and got started to work.

Jane settled into the calming routine of washing, cutting, and styling. She and Rodney told all of their clients about the break-in, Rodney made light of the destruction, saying that he'd been thinking about redecorating anyway. Jane was glad to let their client's words of comfort wash over her as she focused on her work.

Finally at eleven, she had a moment to herself. It was time to call Jeff Hammond and see how soon he was going to get a new site supervisor. There was nothing she could do about Bethany, the break-in, or John and Rodney's relationship, but she could do something about the salon. She'd breathe a lot easier when the work was finished and she could sleep in her

A Discriminating Death

own bedroom again.

Jane settled herself at the consultation table in the empty front room and dialed Jeff's cell number.

"Hammond Brothers." Jeff's voice was rushed.

"Jeff, this is Jane Brooks. I'm just calling to check on the status of a new site supervisor."

"Jane, you are going to have to call back later. I don't have time for you right now."

"Excuse me?" Jane had never heard Jeff talk to her this way. He'd always been the professional part of Hammond Brothers. "I need to know when construction is going to start again, Jeff. It isn't my fault that Mark was so out of line."

"Jane." Jeff's voice rose in irritation. "Did you happen to catch the news last night?"

"I heard a little of it, but I had my hands full yesterday. What's going on?"

"A construction site was attacked by some environmentalist whackos yesterday, major damage was done. The site is one of mine, a big one of mine. Now I'm sorry, but you're just going to have to wait for me to find some time to get you a supervisor that you can work with."

"Jeff, I had no idea that was your site," Jane said.

"It is, and I need you to just back off for a while. You started all this mess and now you just have to wait till I have some time to clean it up."

Jane felt her blood pound in her ears. "Now you listen to me, Jeff Hammond. I did not start all of this. Your brother is a bully and a racist and he's the one who started all of this mess! I am not going to apologize for refusing to put up with his behavior. We still have a contract and I need you to fulfill it. I have a business to run."

"I do too, Jane."

She could hear him take a deep breath and she fought her urge to say something else.

"I'm sorry. I'll do everything I can to help you, but it may take a few more days. Today I have meetings with the police department and a security outfit that is going to be monitoring our site, and I have to talk to the worker's union too. Would it be okay if I called you by Friday to let you know who we've selected as your new supervisor?"

"That would be fine, Jeff." Jane paused. "Why do you think SON attacked your site? Do you think my shop might be in any danger?" The thought of protestors marching around the house she grew up in was too terrible to imagine.

"I think your project is small potatoes." Jeff sighed. "Apparently, they were targeting the downtown site because we're building in an area that was originally zoned as a greenway. The city was the one who voted to allow development and sell the land. SON should be protesting them, not us. They're protesting up at the Restin resort now too. I never thought I'd say it, but thank God I lost that bid. What a disaster." He snorted. "Love your planet, but destroy your neighbor. What kind of philosophy is that?"

"I'm sorry that you have to deal with this," Jane said. "I hope that is the last you see of them."

"Thanks Jane. I'll call you on Friday, I promise."

Jane hung up the phone and looked out the front window. She knew she would have to tell Rodney about the SON connection to their own salon, but she was sure not looking forward to it.

Her phone rang again, startling her. She glanced down, surprised to see John's picture come up on the screen. She turned to make sure that Rodney wasn't in ear-shot before she answered. "John. Any news on the break-in?"

"Jane, is Rodney with you?"

"Yes, well, he's with a client." Jane lowered her voice.

"Do you have the radio on?"

Jane did not like where this conversation was going. "Yes."

"Turn it off. There's going to be an announcement in about twenty minutes, and I don't want Rodney to find out

A Discriminating Death

about it like that."

"Find out about what?" Jane could feel cold waves run down her spine. She didn't know if she could handle one more piece of bad news.

"Sorry, Jane. I didn't want you to find it out like this either. We've found Bethany's body. A couple of boaters saw something floating in the Tennessee River, down near campus. It was her."

Jane closed her eyes and tried not to imagine Bethany's blonde hair floating in the muddy waters of the river. She quickly opened them again and tried to focus on the silk arrangement in the middle of the conference table. "Are you sure? I mean, how can you be sure it's her?"

John paused and Jane wished she hadn't asked the question. "She didn't have any identification on her, but the body is certainly her height and build. The clothing is the same as Bethany was last seen in. Our techs were able to get some partial fingerprints, despite the tissue damage from the water. The prints were a match."

"Oh, John!" Jane felt like crying. "This is going to just kill Rodney. You've got to talk to him. He won't be able to get through this without you."

"Do you think I haven't tried?" John sounded close to tears too. Jane wondered where he was calling her from and if any other cops could see him. "He won't answer my calls. He won't even turn his phone on."

"Talk to him tonight. Or come by here," Jane said.

"Listen, I know he's mad, and I know he's hurt, and I know we have to talk, but now is just not the right time."

"Now *is* the right time," Jane insisted. "Come on, John, you've got to reach out to him. He just can't handle this without you."

"I can't, Jane." John sounded desperate. "I just can't right now."

"What if you don't have another chance to tell Rodney

how you feel? What if this is the straw that breaks the camel's back?"

"Jane, trust me on this. Rodney and I both need some time to cool off before we talk about our relationship. Right now, we would both say things that we would regret. Now, will you please go turn off the radio?"

Jane wiped her eyes with the back of her hand. "Yes, John. I'll turn it off." She paused. "Please, please be careful, okay?"

"I promise. Thank you for helping Rodney with this."

Jane slipped her cell phone into her pocket and stood up just as Rodney and his client walked into the front room.

"Honey, I am so proud of you for getting that promotion." Rodney held the front door open, and a gust of hot air blew into the room. "Now promise me that you'll give me one of your new business cards, okay? I've never had a vice-president of a bank for a client before. The way things are going at our salon site, I just might need another loan."

Jane walked quickly down the hallway. She saw Annie in the workroom and motioned for her to follow. Annie looked confused but laid down the calla lily arrangement she was working on and followed Jane.

Jane turned off the radio and sat in her stylist chair.

"What's going on?" Annie asked as she sat down in the dryer chair. "Is everything okay?"

"Wait on Rodney, and I'll tell you."

"Wait on me for what?" Rodney walked through the doorway. "Tell us what?"

Jane bit her lip. There was no easy way to tell them the news. She might as well just get it out as quickly as she could. "John just called me. He said the police will be making an announcement in about fifteen minutes. They've found Bethany's body."

Rodney held his hand to his mouth and sat down in his stylist chair. Annie jumped up and started pacing the small room.

A Discriminating Death

"Where did they find her? What happened?" Rodney's face was pale.

"Apparently, a couple of boaters found her in the river near campus."

"How did she die?" Annie stopped pacing long enough to look at Jane.

"I don't know, John didn't say." Jane turned to look at Rodney. "John did say that he tried to call your cell but it was off. He called me because he wanted to make sure you didn't hear the news on the radio while you were working. He's concerned about you."

"Please." Rodney waved his hand in the air. "I can't even think about him right now. If he was so worried about me then he would have come by to tell me the news himself."

There was no way that Jane was going to admit she had suggested the same thing to John only minutes before.

"This is just unreal," Annie said. "Poor Bethany. Poor Phillip. I can't imagine what he is going through."

"Yeah, if he had waited on her to leave instead of going home first, she might still be alive." Jane tried to imagine living with that fact for the rest of her life. She did feel sorry for Phillip.

"Remorse for leaving early may be the least of Phillip's problems right now," Rodney said.

Annie frowned at him. "What are you saying?"

"Only that since he was the last-known person to see her alive, surely the police will consider him a suspect. I mean really, we only have his word that she left work after him. No wonder he never made the announcement about running for governor on Monday."

"Phillip couldn't be a suspect! He'd never hurt Bethany." Annie looked outraged.

Jane held up her hands. "Truce, you two." She looked at Annie. "Rodney is right about this. The police would have to consider him a prime suspect since he was the last to see her alive, but that doesn't mean that we think he murdered her. The police wouldn't be doing their job if they let his position and money influence their questioning."

"I know, but really, there's no way that Phillip could have harmed her. He doted on Bethany. She handled everything for him during the funeral arrangements. He's going to be just lost without her."

"I agree with you, I really do," Jane said. "I'd have figured that if any Restin family member was going to be mixed up with the police, it'd be Cindy."

"You've got a point there. Cindy's a piece of work. The police have to know her history with Garrett by now. I bet they're going to check out his alibi too." Rodney turned to Annie. "Garret was Bethany's boyfriend until Cindy stepped in. Phillip gave him a traveling job to get him out of the office, but he could still have his pass to get into the building."

"Ugh. I didn't know about Cindy or Garrett. Still, their security passes weren't swiped so they weren't in the building." Annie frowned. "I guess they could have waited 'til she came out to her car, but anyone could have grabbed her from the parking lot. What are the chances of the police actually being able to find a random killer? I wonder if the police have any decent leads at all."

Jane hugged her arms to her body. "I guess we'll just have to wait and listen for the announcement. It should be on in a few minutes."

"Let's turn on the television in the work room," Annie suggested. "If Phillip makes a statement, I'd like to see him in person."

The front bells chimed. Jane leaned into the hallway and saw her next client. "Come on back, Lucy. We're going to the work room first. There's a newscast coming on."

Lucy followed Jane and Rodney into the small room, picking her way across the floral stems littering the floor. "What's going on?"

A Discriminating Death

"The police are going to announce a break in a missing person case. She was a friend of ours."

"Not the secretary from downtown?" Lucy looked shocked.

Jane nodded.

"Hush. It's coming on." Rodney leaned closer to the little television set.

The conference was short. Jane watched the police spokesman calmly relate the barest of details. The body was found in the river, and the cause of death was strangulation. No suspect was in custody yet, but several persons of interest were being questioned. Anyone with any information should come forward. Jane had heard it all before, and she was extremely doubtful the police were actually pursuing several leads as they claimed. More likely, the police had no idea of where to go next in the investigation. Phillip and Cindy were nowhere to be seen.

"That's just terrible," Lucy said. "I'm so sorry for you guys. Did you know her really well?"

"Well enough," Rodney said. He looked to Annie. "Could you give Jane a ride home tonight? I think I'm going to call it quits for the day."

Jane grabbed his arm. "Are you sure? Are you sure you want to be home alone right now?"

"Yes. I think that is exactly what I want. Do you mind calling my clients?"

"No, no. I'll call." Jane frowned.

"I'd be glad to give Jane a lift. We'll pick up something for dinner and bring it over okay?" Annie looked at Rodney with concern.

"Don't worry about dinner. I don't have much of an appetite." Rodney leaned down and kissed Jane on the forehead, then turned and kissed Annie on the cheek. "I'll see you tonight."

He took off his black work cape and grabbed his car keys

from his station. Jane heard the jingle of the front door as he left. She exhaled; unaware that she had been holding her breath.

"Oh, Jane, I'm so sorry," Lucy said again.

"It's okay. Do you mind waiting for a minute while I call his next few clients?" Jane was worried that not all of his clients would be quite so understanding this time around. Rodney's clients were loyal to a fault, but there was only so much rescheduling people would take before moving on to another shop. Rodney was going to have to start to pull himself together, and it looked like he was going to have to do it without John's help.

"Do what you need to do. I'm not in any rush." Lucy walked to the salon room.

Jane looked at Annie. "I've never seen Rodney so devastated."

"Me neither. I don't know how much more he can take."

Jane rubbed her forehead where Rodney had kissed her. "I just want everything to go back to normal."

Annie picked up a calla lily and twirled it between her fingers. "I have a feeling that's not going to happen any time soon."

Jane walked into the empty front room. Before she called any of Rodney's clients, she wanted to call Brian. Maybe he hadn't heard the news on the radio yet.

She pressed the number three on her phone to speed-dial his cell. He answered on the first ring.

"Oh Jane." His voice was deep and calm. Jane always thought of it as his work voice and realized he had already heard the news.

"I wanted to talk to you about Bethany." Jane's voice wavered. She bit her lip and looked at the waves of heat rising off of the parking lot.

"I was getting ready to call you. I heard it on the radio," Brian said. "I'm so very sorry. How's Rodney coping? Is there

A Discriminating Death

anything we can do for him?"

"He's gone home for the rest of the afternoon. I don't know what we can do for him other than just be there, and let me tell you that it's a damn sight more than what John is doing right now."

"Do you want me to come over tonight?" Brian asked.

"That would be wonderful." Jane sighed. "Oh Brian, it isn't just Bethany's death, it's everything. It's the break-in yesterday and that damn SON group." Jane put her hand over her mouth. She couldn't tell Brian about the John's involvement with the protestors.

"Slow down, Jane. What break-in? What protestors?"

"It's been a hard couple of days. Rodney's house was broken into yesterday. The place was wrecked but not much was taken. We've almost got everything back to normal."

"Are you okay staying there? You and Rodney can come and stay with me if you don't feel safe."

Jane allowed herself to think for just one moment about sleeping in Brian's house before she declined. "No, we're okay. John arranged for police surveillance just to make us feel better. It was pretty terrible though. It's awful to think about someone going through your things, touching everything."

"You and Rodney have had a rough week so far. Now what is this about the SON group? That's the one on the news, right?" Brian paused. "Don't tell me they are protesting your construction site."

"No, but they still could slow us down. The downtown site that was vandalized was one of Hammond's, and they are the contractors for the salon. I talked to Jeff today and he's at his wit's end. He doesn't know when he'll have a new supervisor for us." Jane hated not being able to tell Brian the whole truth. If John had only been honest weeks ago and told Rodney he was going undercover, they never would have followed him in the van and she would be blissfully ignorant of his involvement with SON. She sure wouldn't be hiding things from her boyfriend if John hadn't hid things from his.

"Let's just take things one at a time, okay?" Brian said. "First things first, you have to eat. How about I bring dinner for you guys tonight, say seven o'clock? We can talk more about Bethany, and we can see what we can do to help Rodney deal with this."

"Can you pick up enough for Annie too? She's giving me a ride home tonight. I rode in with Rodney and he's already left."

"Sure thing, I'll grab Chinese and meet you at the house."

"Thank you, Brian. I really do appreciate your help. It's hard to know what to say to Rodney right now."

"There's nothing in the world you can say to make anything better. You can only listen and be there for Rodney. Sometimes, that's enough."

* * *

Jane and Annie arrived at Rodney's house at ten minutes to seven. There was a patrol car parked at the curb, right across from the front door. Jane doubted anyone would try to break in again anytime soon.

She opened the garage door, and Annie followed her upstairs to the kitchen. "Rodney! Annie and I are home and Brian is coming over, so you had better make yourself presentable," Jane yelled into the silent house.

Annie raised her eyebrows. "Do you think he went out?"

"No, I bet he's in the bedroom. He hides back there and stays on the computer. With any luck, he's taking a nap. Lord knows he needs one; he hasn't slept through the night since we followed John," Jane said. If Rodney was asleep, she sure wasn't going to wake him. "Let me go check."

Jane left Annie in the kitchen and walked to the back bedroom. She could hear music coming from behind the closed door. She knocked gently and leaned closer to listen for any movement. Rodney jerked the door open quickly, causing Jane to fall forwards in surprise.

"Were you spying on me?" Rodney put his hands on his hips. "Were you listening at keyholes?"

Jane held her hand over her racing heart. "No! I was not spying on you. I just wanted to let you know Brian's coming over in a few minutes, and he's bringing dinner."

Rodney looked mildly surprised. "You know, I am a little bit hungry. I didn't stop by the grocery store so we don't have anything here to eat anyway."

"I tried to call you and let you know we were having company. It wouldn't kill you to answer your phone once in a while." Jane regretted her choice of words the minute they were out of her mouth.

Rodney frowned at her. "I didn't feel like talking to anyone."

The front doorbell rang, and Jane hurried to the foyer. Annie beat her to the door and opened it for Brian. His arms were full of plastic bags packed full of Styrofoam containers.

"Should we offer some to the police officer?" Brian tilted his head toward the front yard as Annie closed the door behind him.

"I think it would be okay," Annie said. "I don't know if he'll accept, but it wouldn't hurt to ask."

"He won't even accept a glass of ice water." Rodney strolled into the foyer. "I offered him a drink when I got home. I felt kind of sorry for him sitting out there in the heat, but he said he wasn't allowed to take anything."

"More for us, I guess." Brian looked toward the kitchen. "Are you guys ready to eat?"

"Oh yes," Jane said. "I'm starving."

Brian placed the bags on the table and started to unpack the steaming containers of noodles and rice.

"All we have to drink is water or wine," Rodney said. "I threw out everything else after the break in. I even tossed the tea bags."

"I think a glass of wine would be fabulous." Annie grabbed some plates from the cupboard and set them on the table.

"How about a Chardonnay?" Rodney peeked into the refrigerator. "That seems to go a little more with Chinese food than red."

"Chardonnay would be perfect." Brian passed out napkins and plastic forks while Jane got four wine glasses down.

Everyone filled their plates, sampling every dish that Brian had ordered, and then focused on eating for a few minutes in silence.

Brian put his fork down and looked at Rodney. "I heard about Bethany today, and I want to offer you my condolences. It is a terrible loss."

"Thank you," Rodney sighed and pushed some rice around his plate with half of an egg roll. "I don't know how to absorb it. This week has been so hard, and then this last tragedy just will not settle in my brain. I keep forgetting it's real, and then I remember and it's a shock all over again."

"I think it's a blessing that some things take time to become real to us." Brian's voice was low again. Jane watched him in amazement. There was something about Brian that made people relax. "Maybe it's one way of protecting ourselves. I think we know on some level that there's only so much sorrow we can take. Shock and numbness can give us the space we need to grieve in stages so we don't have to deal with everything at once."

Annie took another sip of wine. "Will you be doing her service?"

"No. I'm not exactly sure, but I think that Marshall's Funeral Home is handling the arrangements. We should know for certain soon enough."

Rodney stared at his plate. Brian glanced at Jane and Annie and then turned back to Rodney. "Now, tell me about this break-in that you had yesterday. You and Jane sure have had your share of bad news lately."

Jane glanced at Rodney. Brian made people want to talk to him, but they couldn't afford for Rodney to tell Brian everything.

"The police think it was some kind of random break-in." Rodney reached for the carton of steamed broccoli. "Not a lot was taken, but just about everything was trashed. It took us all night to get things back together."

"Why the patrol car if it was a random break-in?" Brian asked.

Rodney's eyes flickered toward Jane. "Because John's a cop? I guess they get special status."

"They deserve it for all they do for the community." Brian leaned back in his chair, his long legs brushing up against Jane's calves. Jane tried to focus on her food.

"Oh, John does a lot for his community," Rodney said. "It's his family that gets the short end of the stick."

Annie patted Rodney on the back. "You're going to have to talk with him sooner or later."

"That's what I'm afraid of." Rodney pushed his plate away and picked up his wine glass. "Whatever am I going to say when I talk to him? I've gone over it and over it, and I just can't see a way out of this. I can't see any way that I'll ever get over being afraid when he goes to work."

"I can only imagine how you feel." Brian frowned. "John does have a dangerous job, but let me assure you that even if you were married to an accountant, there's no guarantee he wouldn't be run over by a bus on his way to his nice quiet office."

Jane looked up at Brian. She wasn't quite sure how this line of thought was going to help Rodney.

"I've seen such terrible tragedies in my line of work," Brian said. "Life is short, Rodney. You are just going to have to decide what you want out of the little time you have here on this earth. Do you want John enough to deal with your worry and anxiety? Or, do you want some semblance of peace and security either by being alone or with someone else?"

"I'm not exactly sure what I want yet," Rodney said. "I'm afraid that I want John without any risk, and I know that is the one thing I cannot have."

"Brian's right," Jane said softly. "All of life is risk, and you sure don't know when your time is up. My mother was just driving to work on a normal weekday morning when she was killed. It was a terrible way to learn that every single day is a gift."

"It does all come down to the fact that it is *your* life, Rodney," Annie said. "It's your life, and you are the only one that gets to decide exactly you want out of it."

"Then I've got some more thinking to do." Rodney frowned and then swallowed the last of his wine.

Chapter Nine

"Whites left them alone because they were so wild and devil-fired and queer and witchy. If a man was fool enough to go into Melungeon country and if he come back without being shot, he was just sure to wizzen up and perish away with some ailment nobody could name. Folks said terrible things went on back yonder,

blood drinking and devil worship and carryings on that would freeze a good Christian's spine-bone"[x]

"We have got to get groceries, and I mean *today*. I am sick of eating out." Jane frowned at her sausage biscuit.

Rodney sipped his coffee and pulled back out onto Kingston Pike. "I know, I know. I was just too upset to go yesterday. I promise we'll go after work."

Jane couldn't even begin to imagine everything that had to be replaced. Rodney had made a thorough sweep, and the shopping was going to be a major ordeal, not to mention expensive.

"I'll make a list." Rodney parked the car. "But it'll have to wait. My first client is already here. Why on earth does Charlene have to be early for everything?"

"Why on earth do you keep giving her morning appointments?" Jane popped the last of the biscuit into her mouth and stepped out into the heat. She felt her hair wilt as she walked the few feet to the front porch. Today was going to be miserable again. Fall felt like it would never get here.

Rodney pushed the door open. "Charlene! Honey, come on back. I hope you haven't been waiting too long."

Jane's first client wasn't for another thirty minutes, plenty of time to talk with Annie and Grace. She found them both in the work room. Annie was furiously assembling a dozen red roses while Grace filled out dedication cards. Several completed arrangements and potted plants covered the floor.

"What's going on?" Jane stepped carefully over to a stool. "Is there anything I can help out with?"

Annie looked at her and grimaced. "We got a ton of orders online for flowers to be sent to Bethany's mother and to Phillip's office. There's still no news about the funeral date, but if this is an example of the people interested in expressing their sympathy, it's going to rival the Restin service."

"We got a few orders in yesterday afternoon, but we were completely surprised this morning when we checked the website." Grace poked a dedication card onto a floral pick and stuck it into a plant. "We already had to call in an extra delivery from the wholesaler."

"Tell me what to do." Jane grabbed a green apron and tied it around her waist. "I have about thirty minutes now and then another break later in the morning."

"I've got to finish the cards - no offense, but you and Annie have terrible handwriting. Could you make some bows?" Grace nodded toward the row of ribbon.

Jane wasn't offended. Bows were definitely more her speed.

"Did John come home last night?" Annie asked as she picked up a bucket of white carnations.

"Not before Rodney went to bed," Jane sighed. "I got to

talk with him for a few minutes, but I didn't find out anything new."

"Are they still fighting?" Grace stuck another card on a floral pick and looked around the crowded floor for the correct arrangement.

"Yes. I don't know how they're going to fix the mess they're in." Jane pulled out a length of burgundy ribbon. "Especially since neither one is willing to talk to the other."

"Do you think last night helped at all?" Annie asked. "I think Brian did a great job of talking with Rodney. Brian is really very calming."

"Oh, I bet he doesn't have a calming influence on Jane." Grace winked her bruised eye and smiled at Jane. "Quite the opposite, in fact."

Jane blushed and tied off the bow. "I will not discuss Brian's effect on me, thank you very much."

"Then let's discuss Annie's sudden interest in taking the deliveries," Grace laughed.

"What?" Jane looked at Annie.

"Well, since so many arrangements are going to the office, I thought I could stop in and offer my condolences to Phillip in person." Annie stammered slightly as she focused on the flowers in her hand.

"Yep," Grace said. "In the two years I've worked here, Annie has not volunteered to take the delivery van even once. This must be true love."

"I think it's about time." Jane smiled at Annie, who was still staring intensely at a carnation. "Let me fluff your hair before you head out."

The sound of glass breaking echoed through the room.

"What was that?" Jane tossed her bow on the counter.

"It came from the salon," Annie said.

Jane tried not to trip over the mounds of cut stems as she hurried to the salon room. She rushed through the doorway and found Rodney standing in a green pool of disinfectant.

Glass shards and combs were scattered everywhere.

"Are you okay?" Jane peered at him. His face was pale and his hands, still holding the metal lid to the barbicide jar, were trembling.

"What happened?" Annie appeared behind Jane. Grace leaned over Annie's shoulder.

"Be quiet," Rodney hissed. Everyone froze. Rodney walked to the radio on the side table, his feet crushing the glass into the hardwood floor. He turned up the volume and sat down in the dryer chair.

Jane listened as the reporter's voice droned on in monotone. "Police are urging the public to come forward if they have any information on the murder. Next up, your weather forecast looks like more of the same. It's going to be another hot one, folks."

Rodney turned the radio off and looked at Jane.

"Will someone please tell me what's going on?" Charlene demanded, still seated in the stylist chair.

"A security guard at the Restin Resort site was killed last night. His body was found this morning." Rodney's voice was monotone.

Jane met Rodney's gaze. Rodney didn't know that she had spoken with John last night, but he'd seen the blankets on the couch again this morning, so he must know John was safe. Well, John was safe for the moment, at least.

"I'm sorry that startled you Rodney," Jane said slowly. "What a terrible thing to happen." She turned to Charlene. "Rodney and I have had a rough week. Please forgive our case of nerves. Did you know we had a break-in? And did you hear about Bethany Collins? She was a good friend of Rodney's from his college days."

"Oh, honey. I am so sorry!" Charlene said. "No wonder you're a bundle of nerves. Is there anything I can do for you?"

Rodney stood up. "No, no. I'm okay." He looked at Jane. Jane held her breath. He couldn't afford to cancel any more

clients. "Just let me get the broom out and clean up this mess, and then we can get back to your hair."
"I'll clean it up," Jane said.
"No, it's okay. I've got it."
"Come on Grace, we've got a ton more to do before I leave." Annie pushed Grace back out of the door. "Jane, do you mind finishing a few more bows for us?"
Jane glanced at Rodney. "Sure thing, Annie, I'll be right there."

* * *

Rodney did not drop anything else the rest of the day. The only sign that he was still nervous was his insistence that the radio be tuned to news and talk instead of the usual soft rock. Jane was able to tune out the soft rock; she often forgot it was even on. Not so with the talk channel. By four o'clock, Jane didn't think she could listen to one more political analyst or weather report without running screaming from the building.
Annie didn't leave to deliver the arrangements until well after eleven. There were just too many to make for her to leave at the usual time. She still wasn't back by four, and Grace was working at a furious pace to keep up with incoming orders. Jane and Rodney had both worked with Grace through lunch, grabbing Power Bars and Diet Cokes to tide them over.
Finally, their last clients left. Jane picked up the broom and watched while Rodney put his combs in her disinfectant jar. "Are you ready to head to the grocery store?"
"I have to go home first." Rodney grabbed his keys from his station drawer. "It's not yet six. I think I can catch John before he heads to work. I've got a few things I need to say to him."
Jane frowned, her grip on the broom tightened. "Now, Rodney? You want to talk with him now? Are you sure that's a good idea? I know you're upset about the security guard, but

honey, maybe now is not the best time to talk to John."

"I'm upset about a lot of things," Rodney snapped. "And frankly, I'm tired of being upset. Honestly, it's exhausting."

This was going to go bad. Jane wanted Rodney and John to sit and talk, but not like this. Rodney was way too upset to be rational. "Are you sure it can't wait 'til this weekend when you both have calmed down a little bit?"

"I'm sure, Jane. I'm going home to talk to John right now. You can come with me or you can wait 'til Annie gets back and ask her for a ride."

"I'm coming with you, Rodney." She had a feeling he was going to need her.

* * *

Jane's hope that the garage would be empty, John's car long gone, was futile. Rodney pulled into the driveway and opened the garage door, revealing John's car parked in his usual spot.

Rodney took a deep breath and opened the car door. Jane waited for a moment and then followed him up the stairs.

Rodney opened the door to the kitchen. Jane could smell freshly-brewed coffee and looked over Rodney's shoulder. John was putting yogurt and creamer into the refrigerator. Empty grocery bags covered the counters. He looked at Rodney and then tuned back to the refrigerator.

Rodney put his hand on the back of a kitchen chair but did not sit down. "I wanted to have a few words with you before you go out with your SON group to attack some more security guards."

Jane stepped to the side and slowly edged toward the door to the hallway. If there was any way she could get out of the kitchen before things erupted, she was going to do it.

"I'm going to work after I get these put up." John bent down to the grocery bag at his feet and pulled out a block of white cheddar cheese. "I'm tired of eating out. Since you and

A Discriminating Death

Jane appeared to be too busy to do any shopping, I thought I would."

Jane cringed at the sound of her name, but John didn't turn to look at her. She moved closer toward the door.

"We need to talk." Rodney stared at John's back.

John shut the refrigerator door and finally turned to face Rodney. "I only have a few minutes before I have to leave. Whatever you have to say, make it quick."

Rodney walked toward John as Jane glanced at the hallway. "You stay put, Jane. I want you here." Rodney didn't look at her as he spoke.

"You two need to talk alone," Jane stammered as John turned to her. "Really, I can give you some privacy."

"Oh no, that's okay, Jane. If Rodney wants you here, then by all means, stay. I have nothing to say to him that I couldn't say in front of you. He'll tell you everything after I leave anyway."

Jane looked longingly toward the hallway once more and then leaned against the wall.

Rodney reached out and grabbed John's hand. John flinched as if he had expected Rodney to hit him. "John, I know you've heard me say this before, but I really want you to listen this time. Just listen to me."

John put his other hand on Rodney's shoulder. "I am listening."

"Please don't go tonight." Rodney's voice was cracking. "I heard the news about the security guard, and I instantly thought about how it would be to hear some newscaster announce your death and then go on to a weather report. I keep imagining Bethany's body being pulled out of the river. John, life is so short, it's a flash and then it's gone. Please, please, don't go tonight."

"Rodney, now listen to me. Life *is* short. You're right about that. Life is too short to allow a small group of our society to terrorize and kill innocent people. Don't you see? My job is to make sure that fewer 'Bethanys' and 'security guards' end up dead. My job is to help life be longer and safer for everyone."

"I am your partner. I should mean more to you than everyone else. I should be your priority, and I am asking you to not go tonight."

"I love you, Rodney. I do, but I am not quitting my job for you. This is what I do. This is what I am. I'm sorry if you can't understand that."

Rodney stepped back. "Oh, I understand it all right. I understand that you have no idea what love means. How could I have been so blind for so long? You don't love me - you love *you*. You want what you want and couldn't care less about what I need."

"The same could be said for you." John stepped forward, his voice raised. Jane winced. She hoped she wouldn't have to step between them again. "All you care about is how *you* feel about my job, not how *I* feel about my job. You don't care that I love my work, that I'm proud of my work."

"So the fact that you love your job means that I have to endure night after night of terrible dreams? I have to be afraid to listen to the radio or turn on the news? I have to live in fear for the rest of my life because you're proud of your job? John, I'm not going to do it."

"Rodney, there are people who can help you with your anxiety and fear. We have police psychologists who are available to spouses for just this very reason. We can fix your problem."

Jane put her hand over her mouth to stop from groaning out loud. Rodney's eyes flashed and she knew John's words had the same effect on him that they did on her.

"Oh, I am not the one with the problem that needs to be fixed. How dare you say that this is something that I need to talk to a psychologist about - as if it didn't have anything to do with you? You're the one who lied to me in the first place.

A Discriminating Death

I'm not going to put up with it any more. I will not do it. I will not be married to a cop. I want a different life."

John's eyes narrowed. "You know what, Rodney? You've got it. I'm not standing in your way. You want a different life? Well, you're not the only one. Do you think you're easy to live with? You want me to change everything I value just so you feel better."

"Go to hell," Rodney whispered. He turned, yanked open the door to the garage and stormed down the steps. Jane and John remained frozen while they listened to the garage door open and Rodney's car peel out of the driveway.

Jane was the first to move. She let out a deep breath and walked slowly toward John. "Are you okay?"

"Oh Jane, what am I going to do with him?"

"It sounds like you don't get to make that decision." Jane felt like crying. "I think he's serious this time."

"I just wish he'd listen to reason and talk to someone about his anxiety disorder." John sighed as he reached down and picked up the empty grocery bag at his feet.

Jane really did try to bite back her response. This wasn't her fight after all, but she couldn't help herself. "Now John, Rodney isn't the only one that wasn't listening just now. I don't think it's fair to ask him to see a doctor while you aren't willing to change one thing."

"Why not? He's the one that has the problem about my job, Jane. I don't have a problem with it. He's the one that is going to have to deal with his emotions."

"I'd agree with that, except for the fact that you two are supposed to be partners. I would assume that meant that his problems were yours too, or at least you'd have a vested interest in solving them."

"Problems? You want to talk about some real problems?" John turned toward her, his face flushed and angry. "How about the fact that I am neck deep in a group that I am ninety-nine percent sure murdered a security guard last night? Someone beat the man to death with a shovel, Jane. He was almost decapitated, and I have to stop them before they do it again. Now, that is a real problem."

"Oh dear Lord," Jane said. She was glad Rodney didn't know that much detail about the murder.

"We don't have enough proof yet to guarantee a conviction, but I'm going to get it. I'm going to make sure that SON pays for this."

"No matter what?"

"No matter what." John frowned and looked at his watch. "I've got to get going." He paused for a moment. "Could you watch out for Rodney tonight? I mean, I don't want ..."

"I know, John. I'll take care of Rodney. You just take care of yourself."

* * *

Taking care of Rodney was going to be harder than Jane thought. Mostly because she had no idea where he drove off to and he still refused to turn his phone on. She thought about driving around looking for him but figured it was pointless. He'd come home when he was ready to talk. Maybe he was just waiting until he could be sure John had left for the night.

Jane picked up the empty grocery bags and then made an omelet for dinner. At least John had picked up some food and she wouldn't have to order in.

After she ate and cleared the dishes, she wandered aimlessly through the house. She toyed briefly with the idea of calling Annie. There wasn't going to be much that Annie could do about finding Rodney, but she could find out about Annie's visit with Phillip. Jane flipped her phone open and dialed Annie's cell.

"Jane?" Annie sounded tired. "What's going on?"

"A couple of things." Jane realized she was pacing like Annie and she forced herself to sit down on the sofa. "First of all, have you seen Rodney tonight?"

"No. Why would I have seen him? Y'all left way before I got back here."

"Are you still at Bloom's?"

"Yes, I'm still here. I sent Grace home thirty minutes ago, but I wanted to stay and finish a few more arrangements before tomorrow. We had at least forty new orders for Bethany's mother just this afternoon."

"Do you need me to come over?" Jane hoped Annie would say no.

"No thanks." Jane could hear Annie yawn into the phone. "I'm almost through for tonight, but I could use some extra hands if you wanted to come in a little early tomorrow."

"Sure thing." Jane didn't mind helping out in the morning. She'd have gone in tonight if Annie had really needed her. That was what friends were for, but Jane was glad she was off the hook for now. She felt a yawn starting, too.

"Now what is this about Rodney? Did you lose him?"

"He lost us," Jane said. "He and John had a fight, the final one I think, and he just left."

"Oh, no." Annie's voice sank lower. "Poor Rodney. What happened?"

"The whole thing was going pretty badly, but then John suggested Rodney see a police psychologist if he was so worried about John's job. Rodney stormed out and hasn't called home yet. I can't believe John was so stupid. He had to have known how Rodney would take his suggestion."

"I don't know, Jane. It might help if Rodney spoke to a psychiatrist about all of his anxiety."

"Not you, too?" Jane leaned back on the sofa and propped her legs on the coffee table. "I agree it might help at some point, but I hardly think it's fair that John just throws everything at Rodney for him to work out. John has to meet him half-way. They are partners. If he had suggested couple's therapy, Rodney might have agreed."

"I hope they stay partners," Annie said. "It's their lives, and they are going to have to figure it out for themselves. It's hard enough to know what I want from my own life, I sure don't need to be going out and trying to solve someone else's problems for them."

Jane laughed. "My mother used to say that we each had to 'tend our own garden.' I swear, it took me the longest time to figure out what she meant by that."

"What a nice way to put it." Annie yawned again. "I'll make sure and tell Grace to tend her own garden when she starts getting too interested in my business again."

"Speaking of your business," Jane smiled, "tell me about your delivery to Phillip's office. Was he in?"

"Yes, he was. He had a temporary secretary who looked scared stiff, like she was way out of her league. She tried to turn me away when I asked to speak to him, but he saw me and came out of his office to talk."

"What did he say?"

"First, let me tell you what he looked like." Annie paused and Jane could hear the sound of a soda can opening. "He looked terrible, absolutely terrible, and that is something coming from me. I don't think he's slept since this whole thing started."

"Oh man." Jane pulled her legs back to the floor and sat up on the edge of the sofa. "I can't imagine what he's going through."

"Not only is he dealing with Bethany's death, now he has to deal with that security guard that was killed on his construction site. Reporters were lined up in front of the building, just waiting for him to come out."

"The death of a security guard shouldn't reflect on him." Jane tried not to think of how much damage a shovel could do to a man. "If anybody should look bad, it should be the company handling the construction."

"I guess anything is news now that people are talking

about him running for office."

"That's terrible. The press should just leave him alone to grieve for a while, first for James, and now for Bethany."

"Despite everything he's been through, he was still charming and gracious." Annie sighed. "He assured me he wanted to reschedule our date once things settled down."

"That's good news." Jane smiled. "You need a good night out on the town, and it sure sounds like he needs to get out too."

"We'll see. I don't even want to think about it till after the funeral."

Jane felt the floor tremor and heard the sound of the garage door opening. "Hey Annie? I think Rodney's home. I'd better go."

Jane closed her phone and hurried to the kitchen. Rodney stood with his hand on the door handle. It looked for all the world like he had no idea where he was.

"It can't end this way. It just can't."

"You can talk to him again tomorrow, Rodney." Jane approached cautiously as if she were walking toward a skittish horse instead of her best friend. "It's okay."

He looked at her, his face pale. "No, the time is now. It's tonight. I've been driving around for the past few hours just thinking and thinking about my life and I realize that my life is with John. I don't have a life without him. I have to tell him that and it has to be tonight."

"Rodney, John left for work ages ago. You get some sleep and tell him when he comes back in the morning."

"No!" Rodney's voice rang through the kitchen. "It has to be tonight. I told him to go to hell. I'm not going to bed with those being the last words spoken. I'm going out to the resort site, and I'm going to find him and tell him that I love him. I want you to come with me."

"Wait, wait, wait!" Jane held her hands up. "That's not going to happen. Just think this through for a moment. First of all, there's no guarantee that we'll find him out there. Maybe SON has something else going on tonight. Secondly, if we did find him, what would you do? Say he's marching and protesting, are you just going to walk up to him and tell him that you love him? Totally blow his cover? Don't forget that he was actually kissing that woman. She'd be sure to notice you sauntering up and professing your undying love. John would never, ever forgive you."

"What do you think I am?" Rodney looked at Jane as though she were the one with crazy ideas. "Do you think I'm that much of a drama queen? I've got it all figured out. I'm just going to find him marching with a sign, or whatever he does to protest, and I'm just going to wave him over to talk to me. I'll either pretend to be a protestor or I can just hide behind a tree or something and then catch his eye."

"Are you insane?" Jane sat down at the table. "That will never work. Trust me, you do not want to make SON aware of your existence. I mean, not at all. These people are serious. Do you know that they killed the security guard with a shovel? They almost decapitated him." Jane thought of the security guard again. Somehow almost decapitated seemed worse than just decapitated. "And these are the people that you want to go and interrupt while they're protesting?"

"And I'm supposed to let John be with these people after the fight I had with him?" Rodney's pale face lost even more color. "Think about what you're saying, Jane. I am going. Are you coming with me or not?"

"Not. Rodney, I am not going with you."

Rodney looked down at his white shirt and khaki pants. "I need to change into something darker." He looked at Jane, his expression blank. "If you can't go with me, at least help me find the large flashlight." He pulled his shirt up over his head and strode off to his bedroom.

"Damn it!" Jane screamed. "Damn it, Rodney! I'll go with you but I am not getting out of the car. Do you hear me? I am staying in the car!"

***

Ten minutes later, Jane was dressed in black and holding two large flashlights. Apparently, police officers only used the kind of flashlight that could double as a blunt instrument. She glanced at Rodney. He too was wearing all black. He gripped the steering wheel and slid his car between two semi-trucks as he merged onto a bypass that would take them toward the Great Smoky Mountains.

"I can't believe I let you talk me into this." Jane leaned back against the headrest and tried to comfort herself with the thought that Rodney's plan simply had no chance of working. Surely, after the murder, there'd be so many police officers out there monitoring the protestors that she and Rodney wouldn't be able to get anywhere near John.

"I didn't talk you into anything." Rodney smiled. His mood had lifted considerably since they'd left the house. "But I'm glad that you came."

"Oh, Rodney, I still think we ought to turn back. It isn't too late."

"I know. That's the very reason we have to go forward. What if tomorrow is too late? I can't afford to take things for granted anymore, people especially." Rodney reached over and patted Jane's thigh. "I want you to know how much I appreciate you and your friendship. I sure don't know how I'd have ever gotten through this past week without you and Annie to pull me along."

"I love you too, Rodney, which is why I suggest we change the plan. Seriously, if John sees you there, he is going to flip out. Why don't we just park somewhere out of the way and watch the protestors? That way, we can monitor John without him knowing it and then you can talk with him when he leaves."

"Jane, you worry too much. No one but John will even notice me. I promise not to call any attention to myself. And once John hears what I have to say, he'll be so thankful I found him. I know he loves me, even if he's being as stubborn as a mule about this whole thing." Rodney glanced at Jane. "You know what's weird? I'm still actually mad at John, but the risk of losing him, the risk of having our relationship just end like that, trumps the anger. I can love him and be mad at him at the same time."

Jane snorted and looked out the window. She knew all about loving someone and wanting to strangle them at the same moment. It was pretty much how she felt about Rodney right now.

The sky was dark, and Jane couldn't see the landscape as Rodney headed the car toward Townsend and Wears Valley, one of the side entrances to the Gatlinburg area. If it had been daylight, Jane would have enjoyed seeing the rolling farmland turn to steep mountainside, and billboards with black bears playing banjos. She'd always liked Gatlinburg, even the touristy parts. Even as an adult, she'd go to Dollywood with anyone that asked her. She especially liked visiting in the early fall when the trees burst with color and the famous fog hung in the valleys.

"You know, I can kind of see why SON is protesting the Restin Resort," Rodney mused. "It's a shame to lose such a large area of undeveloped land."

"It's right next to the National Park," Jane said. "There's a ton of undeveloped land out there for nature lovers to enjoy."

"Oh, and there aren't enough resorts out there for all of the vacationers who just have to try peanut butter fudge and get a T-shirt with a shoeless, moonshine drinking hillbilly on it? Please." Rodney focused on the curving road that was illuminated in his headlights.

"I understand what you're saying, but I still think that a high class resort on a lake might just be what the area needs.

A Discriminating Death

The focus on local history with the Restin Cabin as a museum is a good idea. I think the resort has a chance to attract some serious money to the area." Jane stretched out her legs. "Anyway, even if you disagreed with the development, violence is sure not the way to get your point across."

"Yeah, but I wonder how open the development commission was to input from environmentalists before they voted to change the zoning? And now John is out there in the dark with the Save Our Nature fanatics."

"First, we don't know that SON will actually be there tonight." Jane desperately hoped that this was true. "And second, if it wasn't here, then they'd be protesting somewhere else. I'm not saying that they're wrong about every development site, but some people just have to have someone to fight against, you know? A common enemy gives them a valid reason to wreak havoc."

Rodney tapped the brakes and slowed down as the road narrowed from four to two lanes. "We're getting close."

Jane looked ahead and saw a long line of taillights. Cars were driving slowly by a fenced area, and police cruisers were parked on both shoulders with their lights flashing.

"Look, there they are." Rodney pointed to a well-lit area beside a temporary construction trailer. The gate was closed, and Jane could just make out a large crowd of people marching in a circle and carrying signs. There was another group of people, smaller than the first, assembled on the opposite side of the road. They were marching in a field and many of them were carrying flashlights as well as signs. The lights bounced up and down as they marched, adding to the confusion and chaos.

"Who's that other group?"

"I guess it's people protesting the protestors," Rodney laughed.

"There's no way you're going to be allowed to stop anywhere near here." Jane rolled down her window as they approached the main entrance to the construction site. "The police aren't letting anyone stop near the crowds." Jane heard shouts of "Love your Mother Nature!" mingling with the shouts of "Go home, Hippies!" A harried young officer was leaning in the driver's window of a car several feet in front of them. Whatever conversation he was having with the driver didn't appear to be going well.

"Just look and tell me if you see John." Rodney slowed to almost a stop, and they both stared out of Jane's window.

Jane scanned the crowd as thoroughly as possible as they marched past the car. "I don't see him, and I don't see that spiky-haired woman."

Rodney leaned so far over toward Jane's side that he was practically in her lap. "I don't see them either." A horn honking behind them made him sit back in his seat. The police officer was red faced, waving them forward.

"What do you think the chances are that Spike and John went to another site?" Jane asked as she rolled up her window.

"No chance at all." Rodney frowned. "If he and that skank are not out front, then they're inside the development."

"Wait, wait, wait! You don't know that," Jane said.

"What other reason could there be, Jane? The only other thing I can think of is that she has already discovered his lies and she killed him before the protests started tonight."

"That doesn't make any sense," Jane said. "Say that SON really did break into our house and learn the truth about John. Surely they'd have confronted him before now. No, he has to be at another site with her."

Rodney drove carefully out of the traffic caused by drivers slowing down to stare at the protestors. He headed on toward Pigeon Forge and Gatlinburg. "No, this is the big deal right now. This is where they are. They have to somehow have already gotten behind the fence." He looked at Jane. "Maybe Spike's plan is to kill John in the development site. That'd sure shut down construction for a while. Apparently the murder of a security guard wasn't enough to stop work for more than a few hours. The discovery of a police officer's body would stop things for days."

Jane knew Rodney had a point, but there was no way that she was going to agree with him. "Come on Rodney, let's just turn around and look again. Maybe we missed them."

"They were marching in a circle, and I saw that freak with the blue hair march by twice. If John and Spike had been there, we would have seen them."

"Okay." Jane paused. "Try his cell again."

"He's had it off for days now. That's why I turned mine off too." Rodney ran his fingers through his hair. "We are just going to have to go to plan B."

Jane was absolutely sure she did not want to hear plan B. "If plan B is to go home and sit up all night and wait on him, then I'm for it."

Rodney flashed her a small smile and then looked back to the road. "Ah, here it is." He pulled into an empty gravel parking lot.

"Moonshiner's Hill and Quilting Emporium? This is plan B?"

Rodney drove slowly around behind the building and parked in the shadows. He turned off the engine, unbuckled his seat belt, and flipped on the interior light. "Plan B is that we go in and get him, and here is how we're going to do it."

During the drive up, Jane had thought that Rodney's plan to catch John's eye while he was protesting was the craziest thing she'd ever heard; now she changed her mind. She was actually speechless. She stared at him while he pulled several folded sheets of paper out from the backseat.

"See? I have a map of the whole development site. I found it online and printed it out after I read that SON was protesting out here." Rodney unfolded the first paper and pointed his finger to a dotted line. "Now, we are here." He held the paper towards Jane's shocked face. "Er, no. Wait." He pulled the paper back toward the interior light and then flipped it upside down. "Okay, we're here."

"We are in another dimension if you think that I'm going to let you go in there and run around in the dark forest looking for John after a security guard was murdered in that very same place last night!" Jane's voice was rising to shrill shriek. She hated when she sounded like this, but could not help it.

"Hush, Jane. You're going to scare the coyotes." Rodney grinned.

"Coyotes?" Jane's pitch was so high that she hurt her own ears.

"No, not really. Just relax. I'm sure most of the coyotes and bears have been so disturbed by the construction that they've moved off by now. We only need to be wary of the two-legged creatures roaming the forest tonight." Rodney's voice dropped. "And they had better damn well be wary of us."

"Really? Why in the world would a murderous group of protestors be scared of us?" Jane demanded. "What are we going to do to them? Shame them into handing John over, assuming, that is, that John is even in there?"

"Let's just say that I am prepared for anything." Rodney pulled up the back of his black tee shirt and turned so that Jane could see the handle of a pistol sticking out of his pants.

"Absolutely not, Rodney! I swear to God that I'll call the police on you right now if you get out of this car and walk into those woods with that gun. You have lost your mind!" Jane was shaking with anger and fear.

Rodney looked at her with compassion, throwing Jane off guard. She expected him to be obstinate and defensive, not sad and calm. "Honey, you just don't understand. While I was driving and thinking earlier tonight, I realized that this is a turning point. I can feel in my bones that this is one of the most important moments of my life. Either I can go after what I finally realize I want most, John in my life no matter what the future holds, or I can choose to run away. I know that if I

A Discriminating Death

run away now, I'll never get another chance to make things right. I'll never again get the chance again to grab what I want out of this life."

"But I am so scared for you, Rodney. You are putting yourself in serious danger."

Rodney started to speak and Jane held up her hand to silence him. "Now listen to me. You are not only in danger just walking around in the mountains after dark, but you risk running into the very people that beat a security guard to death with a shovel. Think about it. They beat a stranger to death because he was in their way. They have even less to lose now that they've committed one murder. If they see you at all, you're dead." Jane glared at him. "There's also the very real possibility that the police have their own people out roaming the woods too. I'm sure there's more of a police presence here than just that harassed cop directing traffic. What if you startle a cop out there and they think you're the killer? You are all dressed in black. How will you look, sneaking around a restricted area while carrying a handgun? Come on, this is just a bad idea all the way around."

"It is dangerous. I completely agree. But it is a risk that I am willing to take. Now, I'm not asking you to take it. I need you back here in the car with your cell phone ready. I can call just as soon as I find John, or if I need to, I can call if I get into any trouble and you can call in the cavalry. Okay? You just have to stay here in the car and be my backup. That's all." Rodney paused. "Now, you know that I'm a great shot. One of the advantages of being raised in the country is learning to handle a gun at an early age. Even John's willing to admit that I'm a better shot than he is. I am going to be okay."

"What if this is a wild goose chase? What if John isn't even in there?" Jane's voice cracked. "What if it's all for nothing?"

"Maybe it is, Jane." Rodney's voice was soothing. "But, at the end of the day, I have to know that I've done everything I can to make things right. I have to know that I did my best to not have the last words I spoke to him be words of hate. Now, can you help me? Will you check your phone and make sure you have a signal?"

Jane wiped a tear from her eye and nodded. There was no talking him out of it. He was going to go in the woods tonight with or without her help. Even if she called 911 on him now, he'd be off running to get a head start. She flipped open her phone and saw that the signal was strong, every bar showing full strength. "My phone's okay. How about yours?"

Rodney pulled his phone from his pocket and flipped it open. "It's fine." He looked Jane in the eye. "I promise to return in four hours at the most. I promise. Remember that construction trail that they made to bring out the graves? I checked the maps online, and if I cut through the woods right here, I can get on that road. I'll make good time getting deep into the site, and I can make a quick search of most of the development. At least half of the property is beyond the lake, and I don't think any construction has started out there. SON would only be interested in the actual work sites anyway. Now, if I am going to be late, I'll call you. If you see anything suspicious, you call me, okay?"

"Okay." Jane nodded.

"I wish I had thought to bring some food." Rodney looked around his car. "There is a bottle of water in my gym bag in the backseat. It's probably going to taste like plastic though because it's been months since I have gone to work out with John. Still, it's better than nothing if you need it."

"I'll be okay," Jane said. "You just make sure you are okay too."

"Keep the keys in the ignition in case you have to leave in a hurry and make sure you lock the doors." Rodney leaned over, grabbed a flashlight and kissed her on the cheek. "Thank you for being my friend, Jane. Thank you for helping me." He opened the car door and stepped out.

A Discriminating Death

Jane clicked the door lock and then turned off the interior light. She could see the outline of Rodney's back as he walked into the woods. Thankfully, the moon was full, and as long as the clouds remained thin, he wouldn't have to use the flashlight very much once he got out of the deep woods and onto the work road. She sure didn't want him to draw any attention to himself.

She listened to the sound of the car engine ticking as it cooled down and thought about calling Brian or Annie. She felt very alone in the silence. No one knew where they were. What if something happened to both of them? She glanced in the rear view mirror but didn't see any signs of other cars.

It was almost eleven now, and Annie would be in bed, fast asleep. Jane didn't actually know what time Brian went to bed - she had only just kissed him, for goodness sakes - but the desire to hear his voice made up her mind for her. She dialed his number and held her breath.

"Jane? Is that you?" Brian didn't sound as if he had been asleep.

"Yes, am I calling too late?" Jane looked at the dark windows in the back of the store.

"No, I'm up working. I had a ton of paperwork to get done." Brian's voice grew cross. "Actually, it was Robert's paperwork, but he conveniently forgot to finish it up before he left out of town again. I swear, when he gets back I'm going to tell him that he either has to stay on top of the billing or hire someone out of his own pocket. I'm sick of doing his job for him."

Jane thought about him sitting in his office, looking more like a banker or a stock broker than a funeral director.

"Sorry to complain to you about my brother," Brian sighed. "Now, you must have a good reason to call me this late at night. What's going on?"

Too late, Jane realized that her fear and loneliness had made her forget that John was still working undercover. She started to cry again when she realized that she couldn't tell Brian the truth.

"Jane? Are you crying?" Brian's voice was calm and soothing.

Jane pressed the phone harder to her ear. "Listen Brian, Rodney had another fight with John, and now he and I have gone to look for him. Rodney thinks that John might be working security at the Restin site, and I just wanted someone to know where we are, you know, just in case." Jane trailed off. It was as close to the truth as she could get.

"Where exactly are you? I don't understand."

"I can't explain everything." Jane cleared her throat. "And I'm sorry that I called you so late at night. There isn't anything you can do, I was just lonely and wanted to hear a friendly voice."

"Jane, if you're in trouble . . ."

"I'm not in trouble." At least she wasn't in trouble *yet*. "It's just that Rodney is convinced that he needs to talk to John tonight. He's finally decided that he wants John back, no matter what job he has. And so, he's gone to find him."

"Let me get this straight. Rodney has gone to find John, and you are somewhere waiting on him? Are you near the actual development site? You know a security guard was found dead there yesterday, right?"

"Um, yes." Jane now really, really wished that she hadn't called Brian. "We're okay. It's just that there are all these protestors out here, and I was just kind of getting freaked out by the whole thing. Sorry if I disturbed you."

"You can see the protestors?"

"Yes." Jane felt sick to her stomach as she lied to Brian.

"Okay." Brian sounded relieved. "Listen Jane, if the protestors are there, then surely the police are there too. If John is working security, then one of the officers can help Rodney find him. You shouldn't have to wait too long. I know some of those protests can get kind of wild, but just stay in your car and stay in sight of other people, and you'll be fine."

Jane looked at the abandoned gravel parking lot and the dark woods. "You're right, Brian. I'm just a little jumpy after everything that's gone on this past week. My nerves are shot."

"How about we do something soothing and relaxing this weekend? Maybe we could try out that new Italian restaurant downtown and then go to a nice boring movie? No death or crime at all?"

"Sounds like heaven," Jane smiled. "Are you free Saturday or Sunday?"

"Robert won't get back in town till Saturday night, so can we make it Sunday?"

"Sure thing, it's a date." Jane hunched down in her seat as a large bird flew silently over the car.

"It's nice of you to be there for Rodney tonight. He's lucky to have you."

"Oh, he knows it," Jane said. "Thank you for talking to me. I feel better," she lied again.

"Goodnight."

"Goodnight." Jane closed the phone and leaned back against the seat. What had she been thinking? She should have called Annie and gotten her out of bed before lying to Brian like that.

The car was getting stuffy. The air was a little cooler up in the mountains, but not cool enough if you happened to be stuck in a locked car for the foreseeable future. Jane turned the key in the ignition and rolled the front windows down an inch. She wanted enough space for some air to flow through, but not enough space for anyone to be able to reach in. She quickly turned the car back off and slid over to sit in the driver's seat.

She scanned the edge of the woods and then looked down at the folded map Rodney had left. She turned the interior light back on and examined the map more closely. It showed the Restin property extended from the Quilters Emporium parking lot to a two-lane road several miles to the south. There was a large lake in the middle of land, almost bisecting the property in two. There was so much land to cover that Jane couldn't imagine Rodney would find anything at all. It would be a miracle if he didn't get lost.

Still, the map showed the future location of the cabins and the tourist centers. Jane could see the dotted outline of the large fence that fronted the site as well as the gate house where the protestors were marching now.

If she was reading the map correctly, the original cabin location and the family cemetery were on this side of the property, between the empty parking lot and the entrance gate. She doubted SON would be interested in either of those areas, they would need to target active construction sites.

Rodney's best bet was to head toward either a clearing near the front of the property where the tourist center and a hotel were going to be built, or towards an area beside the water where the cabins and a water park were going to be placed. Sure enough, Rodney had circled both of these spots and had written a question mark on the top of them.

Jane turned off the interior light and let her eyes adjust back to the natural light of the moon. It seemed Rodney had done his homework. Maybe he'd get lucky and find John after all.

She glanced at her phone display and saw that it was close to midnight. It had been a long day, and it was shaping up to be a long, long night. She turned to get a little more comfortable and breathed in the pine-scented air. The breeze was cooling down the car interior, and she closed her eyes.

She imagined Rodney running through the forest. Surely he wouldn't be foolish enough to actually call out John's name. No, he must be listening as well as hurrying toward the construction sites. She imagined him hiding behind a rhododendron and peering through the moonlight. She imagined a large crow settling on a branch above him and opening its

A Discriminating Death

cavernous beak to shriek, "Boom!"

Jane jerked upright at the noise. She opened her phone and saw that it was now after twelve-thirty. Despite her stress and fear, she'd fallen asleep. She turned in her seat and looked all around the empty parking lot as her heartbeat slowly calmed down.

That was a bizarre dream she'd had. The crow had sounded just like a gun shot. Jane flinched as she heard another boom echo across the mountain. This time, there was no mistaking it. Someone had fired a gun.

Jane opened her phone with shaky hands and pressed speed dial to call Rodney. His phone rang several times and then went to voice mail. She didn't leave a message. She pressed the end button and dialed John's cell. His phone did not even ring; it must have still been off, because she went directly to his voice mail. This time she did leave a message. "John, Rodney is in the Restin development looking for you. I just heard two gun shots, and I'm going in after him." She hadn't realized till that very moment that she was fully intending to go search the woods armed only with a large flashlight. "Rodney is armed, and I hope that it's him doing the shooting. Oh, he's looking for you so he can tell you that he loves you no matter what and he's sorry for telling you to go to hell." Jane closed the phone and looked around the parking lot again.

Rodney was going to be angry, especially if he was the one doing the shooting, but she was going to have to call the police. If she called them now, they'd insist on her staying in the car until they arrived and started to methodically search the mountainside. They may even insist on waiting till daybreak, five hours from now. Who knew what could happen by then? There was no way Jane could guess how far away the gun shots were. She did know that she couldn't stay here in the car and wait for someone else to try to find her best friend.

She bit her lip and made a decision. She would call the police and tell them the truth, not all of the truth, but enough to get them started searching. She took a deep breath and dialed 911.

"911. What's your emergency?"

"My name is Jane Brooks, and I believe my friend Rodney Anderson is in danger. He snuck into the Restin Resort Development site looking for his partner, a Knoxville Police Detective named John Bishop. I just heard gunshots coming from the mountain, and I'm scared for his safety." Jane didn't pause to let the dispatcher speak. "I believe he's searching around the hotel and cabin construction sites, and I'd like for the police to come and find Rodney before he gets hurt."

"What is your location, ma'am?"

Jane froze. This was where things got sticky. She couldn't tell the operator that she was waiting in a car. She would be told to stay put till a cruiser could come and get her. There was no way she could do that. She also couldn't tell the dispatcher that she was trespassing on Restin property, which she fully intended to do in about one minute. She decided her best course was just to say nothing and close the phone.

Her phone instantly rang. She looked at the caller ID and saw it was 911 trying to get her back on the line. She waited till the call had gone to voicemail, and then switched the ring tone setting to vibrate. She slipped the phone in her back pocket and picked up the flashlight. It was about eighteen inches long and weighed several pounds. She was grateful she wasn't stuck with a little mini LED light to search the woods with, but she still wished she had another weapon. A flashlight would be little help against whoever was responsible for those gunshots.

She turned on the interior light and started to search the car. There was nothing in the glove compartment but old insurance cards and a tire rotation log. She twisted around to grab Rodney's gym bag from the back floorboard and saw the cardboard box from "The Cutting Edge" on the backseat. She

A Discriminating Death

opened it and grinned. There, wrapped in the original black velvet, was the six inch pair of blades. She pulled them out of the leather holster and held them toward the light. She had never owned such an expensive pair of sheers. She now understood why Rodney was willing to spend the money. They were beautiful, polished as a mirror and perfectly weighted. Rodney would kill her himself if she damaged his scissors, but there wasn't really an alternative. They were as close to a weapon as she could find in the car. They could not trump a gun, but the fact that she had any weapon at all made Jane feel slightly braver.

Still, there was the problem of how to carry them. She wasn't wearing a belt, so the leather holster was of no use to her, and she was going to have her hands full with the large flashlight. She glanced back at the gym bag. Jane thought she had better take that water bottle too. She twisted around and picked it up.

Jane pressed her feet into the floorboard and raised her hips off of the seat. She tried to slide the bottle into her side pocket but it just wouldn't fit. Well, if the water bottle wouldn't fit, then the scissors would have to. Unfortunately, her pocket was not deep enough to keep the scissors from falling out as she walked. Jane frowned and raised her hips off the car seat again. She pressed the scissors down into her side pocket until she felt the tip tear through the fabric. She twisted again and slowly slid the shears down against her thigh. The pocket was now like a sword sheath. The scissor grip was large enough to keep the shears from sliding down her pants to the floor. She liked the fact that the blades were now hidden, but it did make it uncomfortable to sit for too long. Overall, Jane doubted that would be much of a problem tonight.

She scanned the parking lot before she got out of the car. She hesitated, her hand on the handle, before locking the door. What if they needed a quick get away? But, what if someone decided to climb in the car and hide until they got back? She looked at the woods and listened. The only sounds were owls hooting in the distance. The danger tonight was going to be found in the forest. She decided to leave the car unlocked.

The sound of her footsteps on the gravel seemed to echo around the parking lot as her cell phone vibrated again. She pulled it out and saw 911 on the display screen. They had better stop trying to reach her or they would run her battery completely down. She considered turning her phone off, but didn't want to run the risk of missing a call from Rodney or John. She put it back in her pocket and walked toward the small opening in the trees where Rodney had disappeared a lifetime ago.

The trees blocked a lot of the moonlight, but there was just enough for Jane to pick her way around the undergrowth if she went slowly. She didn't want to turn on the flashlight unless she absolutely had to. No need to alert everyone to her presence. There was not a path to follow, so she just tried to aim herself in the general direction of the gate house and hoped to intersect the work road. The trees seemed to close behind her and soon she was completely alone in the woods.

Alone, that is, except for the occasional vibration of her phone as the 911 operator continued to try to contact her. At least the breaks between calls were getting longer. Jane listened to the rustle of leaves and the sounds of crickets. The night was humid and the forest smelled damp and earthy.

Jane was not really a nature girl. She did like hiking in the Smoky Mountains during the fall when the trees were ablaze with color, but that would always be on a crystal blue day and always on a well-marked path, often with a large picnic lunch. Hiking in the moonlight with all of the night-time animals was not really anything she ever wanted to do. Still, she thought of Rodney and the two gunshots and walked on.

The moon went behind a cloud, and Jane walked right into a small branch. She cursed quietly as she wiped the blood off of a scratch on her cheek. It was time for a break. She carefully

A Discriminating Death

sat down on the ground, making sure to avoid impaling herself with the shears and took a drink from the warm water bottle. Rodney had been right, it did taste like plastic, but it was better than nothing.

The clouds moved, and Jane could see a clearing through the trees. Jane took another swallow of water and stood up. She wanted to take a closer look at the path, but she still did not want to turn on her flashlight. Not only would it light up the sky, it would temporarily blind her. She listened to the woods and then pulled out her phone. She flipped it open and held the screen toward the forest floor. The small light showed what appeared to be a dirt road. She'd been dodging trees while walking beside it for several feet. It seemed to be going in the direction of the gatehouse. Jane had finally found the construction entrance to the cemetery. She closed her phone and stepped onto the packed dirt.

The going was a little easier, but not much. The road was downhill, but it was bumpy and uneven. She fell twice and wasn't able to break her fall since her hands were full of the water bottle and large flashlight. The second time, she ripped her pants and skinned her knee. She tried to wipe the blood off, it, but the slightest touch made her knee hurt worse than her cheek. She considered pouring some of her water on it, but decided she might regret that decision later.

Jane was starting to feel more and more alone. There was no sign or sound of anyone. Her phone had stopped buzzing periodically. She pulled it out of her pocket and was not too surprised to see that she was out of cell range. Her last connection to the outside world was lost. Jane looked around the woods and decided that she would walk for another hour at the most. If she hadn't found Rodney by then, she'd turn around and head back up the mountainside where her phone would work again. She'd call the 911 dispatcher, and this time, she would tell them everything.

She took a deep breath and listened for a moment. She

heard an owl hoot in the distance and remembered how her grandmother always said that the owl was a harbinger of death, come to take departed souls away. Jane had no time for old wives' tales. She continued walking, stepping carefully over the ruts in the road.

She walked for another five minutes before the path ended abruptly in a large clearing. Jane peered out from the protection of the tree line and could see a small iron fence circling the meadow. Jane walked slowly into the open and looked around. She could make out several large rocks in the fenced area and realized she'd found the Restin family cemetery. She breathed a sigh of relief. At least she'd been headed in the right direction all along. For all she knew, she could have been walking right back toward the main road.

She grinned a little. Things were pretty bad when you were actually glad to be in the middle of a graveyard all by yourself at one in the morning. Suddenly, a flash of light shone into her eyes, blinding her. She cried out in fear and held her forearm over her eyes to block the light.

"Jane? Jane is that you?"

Jane lowered her arm and looked directly back into the beam of light. She winced and raised her arm again. "Who are you? Lower your light!"

"What are you doing out here this time of night?"

Jane kept her eyes closed. She recognized the voice. "Phillip? Phillip Restin? Is that you?"

The beam of light shook slightly as Phillip walked closer to her. "Yes, it's me. Who else would be out here on my property in the middle of the night?"

Jane flinched at the anger in his voice. "I'm so sorry for trespassing. I was just looking for Rodney."

"Rodney? What on earth is he doing out here?" Phillip pointed the flashlight down towards Jane's chest. She blinked rapidly to clear her sight.

"He's looking for his boyfriend John. They had a fight, and

A Discriminating Death

Rodney thinks that John is out here doing security detail."

Jane couldn't make out Phillip's features behind the flashlight beam.

"Raise your arms and turn around."

"What?"

"I said, raise your arms and turn around, now." Phillip's voice was hard.

Jane slowly raised her arms above her head and turned in a circle. She tried to keep the panic out of her voice. "What's going on?"

Phillip snorted. "As if you didn't know. Well now, I don't see any blood on you so that means it must have been Rodney that I winged up there on the ridge."

Jane felt her knees start to give way. "What? You shot Rodney?"

"I sure shot somebody. There was blood on the ground but no body when I climbed up to see who was sneaking around on my property." Phillip paused. "Just so you know, I still have that gun and currently I've got it pointed straight at you. You may be my ticket out of this particular mess. Now, slowly put your water bottle and flashlight on the ground and then take two steps backwards."

Jane was having trouble processing Phillip's words. She understood what he was saying but it made no sense.

"Stop hesitating. Do it now."

Jane jumped and then put her bottle and light on the ground in front of her. She carefully took two small steps backwards.

"Now empty your pockets. Slowly."

Jane's hands trembled as she slid them in her pants pockets. Her right hand grazed against the metal of the scissors as she grasped her cell phone. She held the phone up to show Phillip. Her left hand was empty and shaking.

"Put the phone on the ground and then take another two steps back."

Jane lowered the phone to the ground and stepped back again. Her thigh brushed up against a headstone, cool in the heat of the night, and she stopped.

"What else do you have in your pockets?" Phillip stepped closer.

"Nothing, I swear." Jane fought back tears. "I don't even have the car keys. I left them in the ignition in case Rodney got back to the car before I did. Phillip, I don't know what's going on, but we can talk about this and figure it out."

Phillip kicked the flashlight and water bottle away as he approached. He tucked his flashlight under his arm as he reached down and picked up Jane's cell phone. Jane could clearly see the gun in his opposite hand. The barrel was pointed directly at her heart, and it did not waver even as Phillip slid her phone into his pants pocket. With the flashlight beam on the ground, Jane could see Phillip clearly for the first time. His face was gaunt and covered with dirt. His eyes glittered in the moonlight as he looked at her.

"You know exactly what this is about." Phillip's voice grew angry again. "I know Bethany sent my family history to you. I heard her leave you the message, and I know you still have the envelope because I sure couldn't find it in your house. I looked everywhere."

"What?" Jane's voice broke as she imagined Phillip searching through her room, throwing her things on the floor. She tried not to think about Rodney, injured in the woods. "I swear I don't know anything about your family history. I swear I don't know what you are talking about. Bethany was sending us your family tree because she wanted to make you a gift! She wanted it framed so you could hang it in your office."

"I don't believe you. Bethany knew my family's secret, and she sent you the information. I suppose she did it for safekeeping, just in case she needed a back-up copy." Phillip paused. "I hated having to kill her. I'll never be able to forgive my father for that. If he had told me the truth while he could, before he

A Discriminating Death

had that damn stroke, instead of leaving the whole sordid tale in an envelope at the lawyer's office, everything would be different. Instead, Bethany found it, and I had to get rid of her. Too bad she sent it to you. Still, it does seem as if my luck is turning. I've got to finish Rodney tonight, and you are going to help me. He'll come to you."

"Phillip, whatever your family history is, you don't have to do this! We can sort it out." Jane hated the pleading in her voice. She was begging for more than just her life. She needed to stop Phillip now before he came anywhere near Rodney again. "You're a Restin, a pillar of the community. You're a leader and a powerful man. You can overcome whatever this is. I'll help you."

"You got part of that right. I am a leader, I am a powerful man and I intend to stay that way. I'm going to be the next governor of Tennessee and then I'm going to Washington. No one is going to stand in my way. Not Bethany, not that ridiculous security guard last night, not you, and certainly not dear old granddad."

"What does your grandfather have to do with any of this? Your family is like royalty around here."

Phillip raised the flashlight up to Jane's chest again, blocking his face from her sight. "You have no idea what my family is like. I didn't even know what they were like until after dad died. No one else can know either. The Restin name has to remain untarnished, or my future is over before it starts."

Jane glanced around her. The moonlight was still bright enough that if she could get out of the beam of Phillip's flashlight, she could see her way to the woods. However, the ground was so uneven and the trees were so far away, Jane was afraid she'd lose her footing before she made it to cover. "Whatever it is, Phillip, we can talk about it. I can help you. Whatever your family has done can't be that bad."

"Oh, it was pretty bad, Jane. Imagine my surprise when I discovered that my esteemed grandfather murdered his wife after she gave birth to his six-fingered son. Imagine for a moment if you will, how the voting population will feel about the Restin name after they learn that grandfather went back home to his mother for help covering up his crime. She arranged for him to buy a newborn baby boy from an impoverished cousin to replace his heir. Then, that charming matriarchal figure insisted that he write a confession, place it in a tin tube sealed with candle wax and leave it with his pocket watch for her to bury with the bodies somewhere in the family graveyard. It was to be her little insurance policy, just in case her own son decided it would be better if no one knew about his crimes. Granddad insisted that my father never sell the old homestead, and dad always made me promise to keep it in the family. Now I know why. What a charming all-American story, the very values that gave rise to a great corporation. No one would vote for the grandson of a murderer."

"Wait, he killed his wife and son because the boy had six fingers?" Jane had to keep Phillip talking.

"Stop playing ignorant. You've spent more than three minutes around Bethany so you know all about the Melungeons. Poor old granddad met his wife while he was traveling up near southeast Virginia. I've seen pictures of her, light hair and pale skin. She must have seen granddad as her ticket out of there. Her lie caught up with her though, blood will tell. Now I don't really fault him for being a racist, that was just the time he lived in, but the rest of the world won't see it that way. When Bethany brought me the letter, I knew that if I wanted to keep my future I would have to make sure that no one knew about my past."

"Oh, Phillip, I think people will understand. No one is responsible for their ancestor's actions." Jane was still shaking but she tried to keep her voice steady.

"I don't think the public would have forgiven the Restin family for that scandal, but it's too late to find out now. After all I've done, I've got no choice but to keep going. And now,

A Discriminating Death

it's time for us to get going. There was a lot of blood, so I know Rodney has to be pretty wounded, but there's no telling how far he's gotten. Come on. You go first."

Jane's heart felt like it was going to beat out of her chest. "I'm not going with you, Phillip. I'm not going to help you kill my best friend!" She closed her eyes and waited for the sound of the gun.

"You are going to come with me. I thought about just taking your cell phone, but I'm going to need your voice. There's no way that Rodney will come to me, not even if I threaten to kill you. He'll want to speak with you first, and then I'd never get him." Phillip paused, and Jane could hear him step closer to her. She was still afraid to open her eyes.

"Now, that means that I'm not going to kill you here. Oh, make no mistake, I'm going to kill you tonight, and we can do it a couple of different ways. If you walk out of here and help me call Rodney, then I promise you that I'll make it quick, for you and him. You both will not suffer one moment. However, if you continue to be stubborn and make me shoot you through the hand before you walk out of here, then I can promise that you and your friend will die terrible, painful deaths. Do you understand me? A couple of hairdressers are not going to stand in my way."

Jane started to cry silently. The scariest thing was how rational Phillip sounded, as if he was presenting a business deal instead of telling her she would not live to see the morning. He didn't talk like he was crazy; he talked like he was determined. She nodded and cleared her throat. "I understand." She did understand that there was no choice but to leave the graveyard, however that didn't mean that she'd cooperate when she spoke to Rodney. She'd tell him to run and call the police. She might not be able to save herself, but she could make sure he was safe. That is, if he wasn't already lying dead somewhere in the woods, bled out from his wound.

"Good girl." Phillip stepped back. "Now, we're going to

follow the road you took down here. About halfway up, we should get a signal. I'm going to shine the flashlight on the path, and you are going to walk. Don't even think about making a run for it. The woods are too thick on either side for you to get far. I will shoot you. The police will not come. They have their hands full with the SON group, and they won't be able to pinpoint where the shots came from. They might try to find us, but it would take them hours. Do you understand your position here? I'm sorry that it has to be this way, but I have no other choice, and neither do you."

Jane just nodded again as Phillip moved the light toward the trees. Everything seemed too real, too present. She was too aware. She felt as though she could see every leaf on every tree. She could smell the freshly-dug grave dirt from Phillip's desperate attempts to locate the confession, and she could clearly hear the owl again, hooting in the distance. She was a live wire, vibrating in the moonlight. She took a step toward the road and heard Phillip step behind her.

Jane walked carefully between the tire tracks. The flashlight's beam bobbed in front of her. She felt the scissors bounce against her thigh as she walked and she knew that she had to at least try to get away from Phillip. If she was truly going to die tonight, then she would do everything in her power to take him with her.

"Keep going."

Jane kept her mouth shut and focused on the reality of her death. She knew Deborah would be sad, but probably not heart broken. She had Michael, and she'd move through her grief and get on with her life. Rodney would be devastated - that is, if he lived through the night. She thought about Brian and almost sobbed out loud. She was so sure he was going to be the one. She couldn't imagine how he'd deal with her death, but at least he had experience with loss. Annie was ignorant of how quickly the world could change. She'd be hit the hardest of any of them. Not only would Jane be dead, her best friend

A Discriminating Death

lost to a vicious killer, but the vicious killer would be Phillip. If Phillip was caught, Annie would probably never be able to bring herself to trust another person for the rest of her life. If he wasn't caught, Annie would be dating a psychopath.

Jane blinked away tears. Crying would do her no good now. Phillip was going to pay for his crimes, and if he killed her, it would be at least with the knowledge that she had done everything she could to stop him. Jane took another step forward and then threw herself on the ground.

"What are you doing? Get up!" Phillip stopped behind her.

"Oh, I've twisted my ankle!" Jane cried as she reached into her right pocket. "Oh, God, it hurts!"

"You had better get up right now," Phillip threatened. "You are either walking farther up the road or you are dying right where you lay. Do you hear me?" Phillip shined the flashlight on her back, causing her shadow to bounce around her as she sat on the hard-packed dirt.

"Don't shoot, please, Phillip. Don't shoot. If you help me up, I can walk the rest of the way. I promise." She tightened her grip on the scissor handles and pulled them out of her pocket. She pressed the scissors against her chest and sobbed again. "Please, just help me to my feet. I can make it. I swear!"

"Damn it," Phillip growled as he bent toward Jane. "This is your last chance."

Jane saw the flashlight beam fall to the side as Phillip grabbed her roughly by the left arm. She spun around and blindly stabbed upward, the sharp point of the scissors digging deep into his chest.

Phillip shouted in surprise and fell backward. Jane kept her grip on the handle of the scissors and felt them slide out of his body. She leaned forward on top of him and stabbed him again. The flashlight rolled to his side, lighting up his face. His eyes were opened as Jane pulled the scissor blade out, wet with blood, and stabbed him again. She smelled copper and felt her own blood pound in her ears as she imagined Rodney, dying alone in the woods, Bethany, floating in the river, and the faceless security guard beaten to death.

Phillip raised his arm with the gun and Jane swatted it to the side. She heard the gun fall to the ground as she tried to pull the scissors out again. The blade was stuck this time, held tight near his ribs, and Jane was unable to pry it loose.

She looked into his eyes, surprised and wide. She reached into his pants pocket with her bloody hand and pulled out her cell phone. She pushed herself off of him and backed away. She kept her eyes on him while she picked up the flashlight. He was struggling to sit up as she shined the light around the road. She could hear her ragged breath as she saw the light glint off of the gun barrel.

Jane picked the gun up and pointed it at Phillip. Her hand was sticky with blood but no longer shaking. He stopped struggling to get up, the scissors still sticking out from his blood-soaked shirt. He looked up at her with raw hatred. Jane's finger brushed the trigger as she slowly backed away.

"Go ahead and shoot me." Phillip gasped for breath. The scissors rose up and down with every breath he took.

Jane didn't speak, she just turned and fled up the hillside. The panic still hounded her, but a joy was lifting her up and she felt as if she could fly up the road. She ran as fast as she could for several minutes and then stopped, doubled over, gasping for breath.

Jane smelled the metallic scent of the blood splattered on her shirt and covering her hands. She dropped the flashlight and grabbed a tree trunk for support as she vomited bile into the woods. She stood up and wiped her mouth on her upper arm, trying to avoid wiping Phillip's blood against her lips.

She carefully put the gun down on the forest floor, the barrel pointing away from her. She had no idea if the safety was on or off, but she'd bet her life that it was loaded. Jane reached in her pocket and flipped open her cell phone. The screen was covered with drying blood, and she wiped it on her

A Discriminating Death

pants.

Jane could see through the smear that she still did not have a signal. She took a deep breath and closed the phone. She looked up and down the dirt road. Thankfully, the moonlight was still bright enough for her to easily see. She had no idea how much farther she had to go before she reached the halfway point and found a signal again. Everything looked the same to her.

She paused and listened to the night. The only sounds were of small creatures scurrying in the underbrush. She knew that if Phillip was following her, he was going very slowly and would make a lot of noise. She doubted he'd be going anywhere soon. The hard knot of fear in her stomach was not for her safety, now all she could think about was Rodney.

She put the phone in her pocket and picked up the gun and the flashlight. She took one more look around her and then started running up the hill again, stumbling on the uneven ground.

The woods blurred by. Jane ran until she thought her burning lungs would burst. She slowed to a stop and knelt down on the soft underbrush at the edge of the road. She put the gun slowly on the ground again and pulled out the phone. "Please, please, please," Jane begged out loud. She flipped open the phone and sobbed as she saw the bars light up. She had a signal.

With shaking hands, she pressed the number one to speed-dial Rodney. She held the phone to her ear and sat back on her heels. The phone rang and rang before going to voicemail. Jane pressed "end" and then immediately pressed one again and listened to the ringing. She heard his voicemail message and silently ended the call.

John was her next best bet. She hadn't seen any sign that SON members were in the area. Rodney was probably right that they would be vandalizing the sites currently under construction. With any luck, John would have a signal on the other side of the ridge near the entrance gates.

She dialed and waited. She didn't realize she was holding her breath until she heard his voice calmly tell her to leave a message. She closed the phone and held it against her chest.

Jane wiped her tears with the back of her hands and called 911. This time, she explained everything, including the location of the car and the entrance to the construction road. She informed the dispatcher that Rodney's partner, John, was undercover in the area and should be informed immediately of the situation. She only stuttered once while describing how she stabbed Phillip. Jane knew the dispatcher had been rigorously trained to avoid showing emotion, but his voice rose and he asked her to repeat the name of her attacker.

"Phillip Restin of the Restin Family Restaurants. Yes, it is most definitely him." Jane paused, and the dispatcher remained silent for a moment. "Now listen to me, he's not the important one here. My best friend Rodney is injured and lost in the woods. I want every available officer out here to help as soon as possible." Jane's voice finally broke. "Please, please help me."

"We are going to do everything that we can. You just remain where you are and an officer will be on the way. We will use the GPS on your phone to locate you and get you emergency help."

"I don't need help," Jane growled, startling a small animal out of the brush. "I'm fine. Rodney needs help. Now, I am going to hang up and start walking back up the road."

"Ma'am, do not hang up the phone. I need you to stay on the line until help arrives."

Jane fought to keep her voice calm. "I'm going to hang up the phone and walk towards the car. If Rodney is able to walk, he'll be headed for the car too. I will call you back every ten minutes to report my location. I sure don't want an officer to mistake me for Phillip or a bear."

"That's not a good -"

A Discriminating Death

Jane closed the phone with a snap and stood up. The adrenaline that had soared through her veins was starting to wear off. Her heart was still beating hard against her chest, but her feeling of flying was gone, replaced by icy fear. She had to find Rodney.

She tucked the flashlight under her arm and gently picked up the gun. She wished she could put it in her pocket, but was afraid that if she fell down again, it would go off. The last thing she needed was to shoot herself in the foot, so to speak, so she carried it pointed toward the ground in her left hand while she pressed speed dial to call Rodney again.

She alternated focusing on the uneven road and focusing on the phone pad as she made her way up the mountain. After ten minutes, she paused and dialed 911 again.

"I've made it further up the path but I still have a while to go before I reach the car. I'll call again in ten more minutes." She didn't give the dispatcher a chance to respond before she hung up the phone.

She dialed Rodney again and continued walking.

The breeze shifted and blew Jane's bangs into her face. She heard the soft notes of Ode to Joy as the warm wind enveloped her. She gasped, and the music stopped as Rodney's voicemail picked up again.

Jane fought the urge to call out for him. It was just possible that Phillip was following after all, and it seemed that the ring tone actually came from slightly behind her, closer to Phillip than to the parking lot. Jane tilted her head and dialed again.

Instantly she heard the music. She started shaking in relief and headed off of the path toward the sound. She'd found him at last. She pushed the thought from her mind that Rodney was still not answering, maybe not able to answer. Rodney's voicemail picked up, and the music went silent again.

Jane continued dialing and hunting for the sound. It was getting louder each time she called. Finally she dared calling his name, softly at first and then louder and louder. She pushed her way through the brush and saw him.

He was lying on his side facing away from her. His pale skin glowed in the moonlight, and Jane realized that he had taken off his shirt. The reason for it was apparent when Jane rolled him over. His shirt, now soaked in blood, was tied tightly around his left thigh.

Jane felt for his pulse, her hands shaking as she stroked his throat. He was still alive. His heart was still pumping. She gently felt his thigh, and her hand came away wet with blood. Jane stripped off her shirt and folded it in two before gently sliding it under his leg and laying it over his make-shift bandage. She tied it as tightly as she dared. She wanted to stop the bleeding but not totally cut off his circulation.

Jane's phone rang out from the ground where she had dropped it. She picked it up, covering it once again with blood. It was 911.

Jane was able to control her breathing long enough to tell the dispatcher Rodney's condition. She tried to give them some clue to their location, but since leaving the trail, she was completely turned around.

"Just stay on the phone with me, and I promise you help will be there soon. The police are out in your area now, and they are using flashlights and bull horns. You just tell me when you can see or hear them coming, and I can let them know when they're headed the right way."

Jane nodded, and realizing that the dispatcher could not see her, said, "Okay." She cradled the phone between her ear and shoulder as she reached down and held Rodney's hand. The dispatcher continued to talk to her, low and soothing, asking questions every few minutes about Rodney's condition. She guessed he wanted to make sure she was still listening and had not gone into shock.

Jane was checking Rodney's pulse again when she heard someone shouting her name. She jumped to her feet and spun around.

"I can hear them!" she shouted into the phone. "I can hear them!"

The dispatcher sounded relieved. "I'll let them know."

"Here! We're here!" Jane shouted over and over again. She shouted until two officers broke through the underbrush. Then, she cried.

Chapter Ten

"To be a Melungeon descendant today is to recognize one's multi-ethnic heritage, and the fact that one's ancestors faced some degree of discrimination for being non-white in a racist society. That recognition will probably lead to a fuller understanding of America's tumultuous history of race relations and the absurdity of the concept of race in general. And in recognizing the difficulties faced by our ancestors, we can also celebrate their perseverance, their determination, and their drive for a better future that allows us to celebrate a heritage that they could note even acknowledge. Simply having Melungeon heritage does not make one a better person, but understanding the ramifications of that heritage my well do so."[xi]

"I can't believe he's really dead." Jane looked down at her lap. The green scrubs she was wearing were a little too small for her and she could feel a seam pressing into her thigh. She squeezed Brian's hand harder and looked at John and Annie, their faces ashen in the harsh fluorescent lights of the hospital waiting room. "I knew he'd lost a lot of blood, but I never really thought he'd die."

"Why didn't you shoot him?" Annie asked.

Jane dropped Brian's hand and rubbed her eyes. She was exhausted and it was hard to think straight after answering question after question from the doctors and the police. "Truthfully, I guess I didn't shoot him simply because he asked me to do it. If he'd begged me to not shoot him, I just might have pulled the trigger."

John looked at her, his eyebrows raised. "Please, don't ever tell that to anyone else, okay? All that matters right now is that you acted in self-defense. Thank God you didn't shoot him. It's one thing for him to die from stab wounds inflicted during a struggle, it would be quite a different story if you'd shot a wounded and defenseless man while you were standing several feet away."

"Things are going to be hard enough for a while. I can't imagine what we would have to go through if you were charged with homicide." Brian's voice was flat.

Annie blinked back tears and looked towards the window.

"That would complicate things," Jane said. It wasn't as if things weren't complicated enough. She had hurt everyone tonight. Not only had Jane stabbed Phillip and left him to die in the woods, she felt responsible for Annie's broken heart. She was ashamed that she hadn't told Brian the whole truth, and she knew it would take a while for him to trust her again. She'd disappointed John. She had promised to look after Rodney for him, and now here they were in a hospital waiting room with a uniformed officer guarding the doorway. The officer's presence was more to keep the reporters out than to keep her and her friends in, or at least that was what Jane hoped.

The reporters had swarmed the hospital. This was the biggest news story they'd had in ages. When the ambulance doors had opened at the ER entrance, Jane had seen reporters crawling over each other, hands clutching microphones and cameras raised over their heads, trying to get a photo or a quote. She was pretty certain that she and Rodney were going

A Discriminating Death

to make the front page. It wasn't everyday you got a blood-soaked victim and killer in the same shot.

Rodney had been whisked away to surgery while Jane was thoroughly checked out by a young doctor. Her cuts and scrapes had been cleaned and covered, and she'd been given Tylenol for the pain. Next up was the police interview. Thankfully, John had arrived by then and had convinced the lead detective to interview Jane at the hospital so she could be there when Rodney got out of surgery. Jane had told her story twice to the detective and his video camera. She was given a sausage biscuit and a cup of coffee from the hospital cafeteria after the interview.

By the time Jane got up to the surgical waiting room, Annie and Brian were waiting with John. John had called them with the news and they had driven right over. They were able to avoid the gauntlet of reporters at the hospital entrance by sneaking in through the morgue. Brian knew a night shift supervisor who was happy to help them evade the journalists.

Brian had enveloped Jane in a silent hug. Annie had cried when Jane apologized to her, stumbling over her words as she told Annie the truth about Phillip. Annie kept repeating that she had no idea Phillip could do anything like that, no idea at all. Every few minutes, she would reach out and touch Jane on the arm, as if to make sure she was actually there.

John hadn't lost the haunted look he'd worn since Jane first laid eyes on him before the police interview. He'd not been allowed to see Rodney yet. Jane knew he wouldn't rest until he could speak to Rodney himself.

John had indeed been in the woods with Helena, the spiky-haired leader of the local SON branch. He had enough to charge her with vandalism and trespassing, but he was absolutely convinced that a SON member killed the security guard. There was no way he was leaving without some proof.

Although John had cell service up on the main ridge near the construction sites, he'd refused to answer his phone. In fact, he admitted being angry that Rodney would even think about disturbing him at work. He wouldn't even answer the call from Jane, thinking that Rodney had put her up to it.

John cried when he told them that he finally answered the next call because it was his boss. She was the one who told him about Rodney. He listened to the voice mail Rodney had left and realized that the slurred and confusing message may have been the last thing Rodney ever said to him on this earth. Rodney had rambled on about a gun shot and said he was thirsty and then he had just trailed off. There was a moment of silence and then the call ended. John had taken off running towards the construction site's front gates, leaving a confused Helena behind him.

Jane hoped she'd never have to hear Rodney's voice mail for herself. She couldn't imagine what Rodney had been through, injured and running from an unknown shooter. It was a miracle that he was even able to make it back up the ridge to call for help. He'd lost so much blood that he finally just collapsed wounded and disoriented in the woods. If he hadn't tied his shirt around his leg, Jane doubted he would have survived.

"Do any of you want another cup of coffee?" John stood up and tossed his cardboard cup into the trash.

"No thank you." Annie leaned back in her chair and looked up at the ceiling. Brian shook his head and reached out for Jane's hand again.

"I'm fine," Jane said. It wasn't true, of course - she didn't think she would ever really be fine again. She had killed a man, and she couldn't get her mind to quite comprehend that. She didn't feel guilty exactly; he had been going to kill her and her best friend just to save his reputation. She thought he probably deserved the fate he got, but still, it had been her hand that had stabbed him, her hand that had been covered in his blood. She wondered if she'd ever be able to forget the feeling of actually pushing the scissors into his chest.

A Discriminating Death

A short woman in blue scrubs walked into the room. Annie rose to her feet and stood beside John.

"I'm glad to report that your friend is out of surgery and doing very well in recovery. We had to give him several pints of blood to replace what he lost, but all things considered, he's a very lucky man. The wound was on his lateral thigh and missed his femoral artery. He's going to be on crutches for a while, but I think he'll heal nicely."

"Oh, thank you," Jane said. She felt like she could finally breathe again.

"When can we see him?" John's voice broke. Annie placed her hand on his back.

"We'll get him set up in a private room after he's finished in recovery. It'll probably be another half hour and then you can go in. He may not be awake, but you can at least see him."

"Thank you." John nodded and then sat down again as the surgeon left. "I don't know what I would do if he had, if he had ..." John couldn't finish the sentence. Jane reached out and patted his leg.

Annie took a deep breath. "I am so sorry I ever let that monster into our lives. I'll never forgive myself."

"Annie, this is not your fault!" Jane frowned. "You didn't have anything to do with this. There's no way that you could've guessed what he was capable of."

"Really, Annie, no one could have seen this coming," Brian said. "No one would have believed Phillip could do something like this."

"Unfortunately, you're right," John said. "It's going to take a lot to convince most of Knoxville that Phillip was anything other than a successful businessman and philanthropist. You are going to be under a lot of scrutiny for a long time, Jane."

"What? Jane acted in self defense! No one could think she set out to kill him." Annie protested. "She had no choice."

"There won't be any official charges brought against her. But it is too bad that we only have her report of the events in the woods. Rodney won't be able to identify who shot him. On the positive side, we do have Phillip's fingerprints on the gun, and I'm sure there will be gunshot residue on his hands. There could also be DNA evidence on the shovel he used to kill the guard, and I know the police are going to turn over every rock in that graveyard till they find the bodies of Phillip's grandmother and her child. Even if James's written confession has turned to dust, there should still be enough for the police to piece together the truth." John turned to look Jane in the eyes. "Still, no matter what details come out, it'll take a lot of time for you to lose the reputation as the woman who killed the Barbeque King."

"Once people find out what he did, they'll be running to distance themselves from him. Give it a couple of months and no one will even be willing to admit they ever knew him." Brian said.

"People are always willing to think the worst of others." Annie stood to look out the window at the media circus three stories below.

Jane stood beside her and watched as another television van set up in the parking lot. "Phillip thought that people would always believe the worst too. He was probably right."

"I don't know," John said. "If he had a good spin doctor, this whole thing could have been avoided. He could have gone on to be the people's choice despite his family history."

"Not likely." Annie pressed her forehead up against the glass. "The business would be ruined. The Restin family name will always be associated with prejudice and murder. That's no way to win an election."

"Oh, just imagine what Cindy is going to think," Jane said. If Cindy had been worried about living down her reputation as a pork princess, this was just going to kill her.

"She's going to be out for you." Brian frowned. "You're really going to have to watch yourself, Jane. I'm serious, no talking to the press or anyone for that matter. If she gets the

A Discriminating Death

chance to sue you for libel or slander, she'll take it."

"No talking to the press is more than good advice." A woman's voice rang out from the doorway. "It's an official order."

Jane and Annie turned to see a blonde woman in a navy suit staring at them. Despite the early hour, she was perfectly dressed, not one hair out of place.

"Sergeant Wilcox." John nodded at her.

"Detective Bishop. I need to speak with you but I wanted to wait until you found out about your partner. I'm glad he's going to be okay." She gestured toward the hallway. "There's an empty patient room a few doors down. We can talk in private there."

"Good." John's voice was firm. "I need to speak with you also." He followed her out of the room past the officer guarding the doorway.

"I hope John isn't in trouble." Jane frowned. "He did blow his undercover assignment. I hope they can still at least press some charges against SON."

"He'll sort it out. I don't think anything can rattle him now he knows Rodney's going to be okay," Annie said.

Jane felt as if she could curl up in the floor and sleep for a thousand years. All of her adrenaline had finally worn off, and from the feel of it, the caffeine had worn off too. She sat in the plastic chair and wiggled to get comfortable. "It's amazing how things could have gone so very wrong in the first place."

Annie started pacing the small room. "I can't believe how the ignorance and stupidity of people two generations ago almost cost me my best friends. To think that it started with a Melungeon woman lying about her heritage and ended with three deaths."

Jane's eyes had closed but flickered open at the bitterness in Annie's voice. "I guess all of our actions have consequences, some we may never know."

John walked back into the room. He was actually smiling a

little bit as he sat down beside Jane. "Stop pacing, Annie. Everything's okay."

"What did she want to talk to you about?" Brian asked.

"She told me they had decided to go ahead and arrest Helena on the vandalism charge. It was all they could get on SON this time around. I asked for a permanent reassignment from undercover. I'll never again be in a position where I can't tell Rodney what I am working on or where he can reach me." John grinned. "She okayed my transfer to homicide. Rodney can't be too upset with that. The crime will have already been committed by the time I get on the scene."

"That's one way of looking at it," Jane said. "Let's see if Rodney feels the same."

An orderly peered nervously past the entrance. "Are you ready to see Mr. Anderson? He's out of recovery and set up in his room. Do you want me to take you to him?"

Jane looked at her friends and smiled for the first time that morning. "There's nothing we would like more."

Epilogue

"He looks pretty good, doesn't he?" Jane nodded towards Rodney.

"You look pretty good yourself." Brian smiled as he put his arm around Jane's waist. "Are you ready?"

Jane looked around at the large crowd of friends and clients that were gathered on her front lawn. It was a perfect October day. The sky was crystal blue, and the leaves had just started to turn. Annie had decorated the front of the salon with pumpkins and fall wreaths. A tent had been set up to house the refreshment tables. Rodney was sashaying around the crowd, laughing and greeting everyone by name. John and Annie were standing by the front door drinking champagne.

"I'd say I'm about as ready as I can get. Let me tear Rodney away from his audience and we can reveal the name of the salon. Annie and John are already in position to pull down the sign cover."

"I can't believe you were able to keep it a secret this long." Brian smiled. "Actually, I can't believe that Rodney was able to keep it a secret this long. He may be out there mingling and telling everyone the news right this very minute."

"He'd better not be!" Jane laughed. She spotted Rodney

talking with Grace and her fiancé by the driveway. Annie had actually closed Bloom's on a Saturday so that she and Grace could attend the grand opening. Jane caught Rodney's eye and waved for him to come to the front.

He was smiling as he walked, not even a trace of a limp now. He claimed his quick healing was from all of his good living. John claimed the speedy recovery must have been due to some strange mixture of salt and vinegar potato chips, gummy bears and hours of daytime television.

"Are you ready?" Jane grabbed his hand.

"Absolutely," Rodney said. He cleared his throat and raised his voice. "Ladies and gentlemen, thank you for attending the grand opening of our salon. It has been quite an adventure getting here, but finally, today is the day. Now I know most of you did your best to help us name our new business, and we really appreciate your suggestions. However, I regret to inform you that we did not ultimately pick one of the suggestions for the name of the salon. No one will win the gift certificates, but we and Bloom's will be passing out ten-percent discounts on future services before you leave."

Jane laughed thinking of some of the suggestions in the box. She had actually liked the name 'Curl up and Dye,' but figured it would not really be in good taste after the events of the past few weeks.

"And now, finally we are ready to open the doors to the salon that will be the very best in town, the salon where you will come and find relaxation, the salon where you will discover just how beautiful you really are, and the salon where your friends are always happy to see you." Rodney waved toward the front doorway.

Annie and John each grabbed a corner of the cloth covering the sign and pulled. The crowd pressed closer to see the words 'The Salon' hand painted in cursive script on the wooden sign. Laugher floated up from the gathering on the lawn.

A Discriminating Death

"Open the doors! Come on in and see for yourselves," Jane said. "Please pay particular attention to the bathroom fixtures and make sure to tell Rodney what a good job he did selecting them."

Rodney nudged her in the ribs as Annie opened the door and ushered people into the main room. "Let's go find some more champagne and toast again."

Melungeon-Related Surnames[xii]
(North Carolina, Virginia, Tennessee, Kentucky)

Adams, Adkins, Barker, Barnes, Beckler, Belcher, Bell, Bennett, Berry, Biggs, Bolen, Bolton, Bowlin, Bowling, Bowman, Branham, Brogan, Bullion, Burton, Byrd, Campbell, Carrico, Carter, Casteel, Caudill, Chavis, Clark, Coal, Coffey, Cole, Coleman, Coles, Colley, Collier, Collins, Collinsworth, Colyer, Counts, Cox, Coxe, Crow, Cumba, Cumbo, Cumbow, Curry, Davis, Denham, Dooley, Dorton, Dula, Dye, Ely, Evans, Fields, Freeman, French, Gallagher, Gann, Garland, Gibson, Goins, Goings, Gorvens, Gowan, Gowen, Graham, Gwinn, Hall, Hammond, Hendricks, Hendrix, Hill, Hillman, Hopkins, Jackson, Keith, Kennedy, Kiser, Lawson, Lopes, Lucas, Maggard, Maloney, Martin, Miner, Minor, Mizer, Moore, Morley, Mosely, Mozingo, Mullins, Nash, Niccans, Noel, Orr, Osborn, Osborne, Perry, Phelps, Phipps, Polly, Powers, Pruitt, Ramey, Rasnick, Reaves, Reeves, Rice, Riddle, Rivers, Roberson, Robertson, Sexton, Shephard, Short, Sizemore, Stallard, Stanley, Steel, Swindall, Tackett, Taylor, Tipton, Tolliver, Turner, Vanover, Watts, White, Whited, Williams, Willis, Wilson, Wright, Wyatt

About the Author

Susan Dorsey is the author of *A Civil Death*, the first in the Jane Brooks series. She lives in East Tennessee with her husband and two children. She is currently hard at work on her third novel. Learn more at susandorseybooks.com and follower her blog www.sjdorsey.blogspot.com

Bibliography

[i] Edward T. Price, "The Melungeons: A Mixed-Blood Strain of the Southern Appalachians," *The Geographical Review* 41 (April 1951).

[ii] Burnett, Swan. "A Note on the Melungeons." *American Anthropologist 2* (October 1889): 347.

[iii] Wayne Winkler, Walking Toward the Sunset, (Mercer University Press, Macon, Georgia), 246.

[iv] James Aswell, God Bless the Devil, (University of NC Press).

[v] Worden, W.L. "Sons of the Legend." *Saturday Evening Post,* 18 October 1947.

[vi] Will Allen Dromgoole, "A Strange People," *Nashville Sunday American,* 14 September 1890, 10.

[vii] Brewton Berry, *Almost White* (New York: Macmillan, 1963) vii, 9.

[viii] Aswell, James. *God Bless the Devil,* Federal Writers Project. Chapel Hill: University of North Carolina Press, 1940. 207-214.

[ix] Dromgoole, "The Malungeons," 472.

[x] *James Aswell, God Bless the Devil,* Federal Writers Project. Chapel Hill: University of North Carolina Press, 1940. 212.

[xi] Wayne Winkler, Walking Toward the Sunset, (Mercer University Press, Macon Georgia). 256

[xii] N. Brent Kennedy, *The Melungeons The Resurrection of a Proud People*, (Mercer University Press, Macon Georgia). 172.

Made in the USA
Charleston, SC
29 April 2012